UNDER
GLASS

A *BOOKLIST* TOP TEN FIRST NOVELS FOR YOUTH

"Jaclyn Dolamore expertly captures the essence of the perfect gothic romance on every page." —Carrie Ryan, author of *The Forest of Hands and Teeth*

★ "Dolamore successfully juggles several elements that might have stymied even a more experienced writer: intriguing plot elements, sophisticated characterizations, and a subtle boost of girl power; it's the women of the tale who have ingenuity, courage, and the power to turn events." —*Booklist*, starred review

"Debut author Dolamore draws heavily on *Jane Eyre* and its themes of sexual and class prejudice for her plot, reshaping the source material with skill." —*PW*

"Mixed into this stunning debut novel are enough plot points to keep readers interested. With touches of steampunk, romance, fantasy, and mystery, there is a little something for everyone." —*SLJ*

"Libba Bray's Gemma Doyle meets Sally Gardner's *The Red Necklace*, with a hint of *Jane Eyre* thrown in for good measure, in this vivid and rousing debut." —*Kirkus Reviews*

"Sorcerers, fairies, ghosts, music, mystery, intrigue—what more could one ask for in a gothic-style fantasy romance? . . . This well-written, engaging work will hold readers from beginning to end." —*VOYA*

"The book offers plenty of romance and intrigue, and readers not quite ready for the weight of Libba Bray's Gemma Doyle trilogy may do well to start here. —*BCCB*

BOOKS BY JACLYN DOLAMORE

Magic Under Glass
Between the Sea and Sky

MAGIC UNDER GLASS

JACLYN DOLAMORE

BLOOMSBURY

NEW YORK BERLIN LONDON SYDNEY

First published in the United States of America in January 2010
by Bloomsbury Books for Young Readers
Paperback edition published in May 2011
www.bloomsburyteens.com

For information about permission to reproduce selections from this book, write to
Permissions, Bloomsbury BFYR, 175 Fifth Avenue, New York, New York 10010

The Library of Congress has cataloged the hardcover edition as follows:
Dolamore, Jaclyn.
Magic under glass / by Jaclyn Dolamore. —1st U.S. ed.
p.   cm.
Summary: A wealthy sorcerer's invitation to sing with his automaton leads seventeen-year-old
Nimira, whose family's disgrace brought her from a palace to poverty, into political intrigue,
enchantments, and a friendship with a fairy prince who needs her help.
ISBN 978-1-59990-430-6 (hardcover)
[1. Magic—Fiction. 2. Robots—Fiction. 3. Singers—Fiction. 4. Wizards—Fiction.
5. Princes—Fiction. 6. Fantasy.] I. Title.
PZ7.D6975Mag 2010   [Fic]—dc22   2009020944

ISBN 978-1-59990-587-7 (paperback)

Book design by Danielle Delaney
Typeset by Westchester Book Composition
Printed in the U.S.A. by Quad/Graphics, Fairfield, Pennsylvania
1 3 5 7 9 10 8 6 4 2

To Dade, who believed in me from the day we met

MAGIC UNDER GLASS

1

The audience didn't understand a word we sang. They came to see our legs. As the posters said,

TROUSER GIRLS
FROM THE
EXOTIC LAND OF TASSIM!

We were billed just under the acrobats and the trained dogs.

Our voices joined in harmony while Saraki plucked the *tei-tan* and I pranced around the stage, my slippers whispering on the wooden floor. My hands curved and wove and paused, each gesture as familiar to me as the words I'd heard my mother sing while I was still in the cradle. I'd done six shows a week in this dank music hall since I'd stepped off the ship that carried me away from home three years ago.

Even before I finished the last plaintive note, a few men began to whistle, and one shouted something I chose to ignore. Boys on the balcony shelled chestnuts, occasionally tossing one onto the people below. Clusters of boardinghouse girls in tatty straw hats giggled.

Through it all, my gaze was drawn to a tall hat in the crowd and the pair of dark eyes beneath it. A gentleman.

He stood in the back, his face still turned halfway to the door, like he had just slipped in for a glimpse and wouldn't stay long. Among all the dim faces that watched me, I kept my focus on him alone.

Saraki let the applause wane and then began to shake her pick across the *tei-tan*'s strings, bringing forth a tense melody.

The program held no surprises. "The Dragon Maiden's Revenge" had followed "Gathering Flowers for My Sister's Wedding" in every show we'd done this year. Still, I hoped I looked very noble as I pantomimed taking up the sword of the fallen king of dragons. Was the gentleman in the back—*my* gentleman—watching?

Yes. Looking right at me, in fact.

Fifteen years ago a railroad baron had married the most famous of trouser girls, Little Sadi, back when our song and dance had been the fashion, before they even called us "trouser girls." Saraki dreamed of following in her footsteps, charming some rich man into whisking her away. I scoffed when she spoke of it, but late at night I dreamed of things I scoffed at by the light of day.

When I finished my song, my gentleman lingered. The raucous crowd around him whooped, but he kept still, his eyes roving over our crude set: a painted village house on a piece of wood shorter than Saraki, and some dried flowers in mismatched vases.

Our last number, "The Fairest Blossom in a Maiden's Heart," had been my mother's signature song. She had performed it at the king's coronation, as a new bride of seventeen, just my age now. The song was an ode to a lover who had died, never to be forgotten. I could never help but remember Mother, her haunting voice pitched high, her delicate gestures transforming her into the very embodiment of sorrow. Her performance had always left the audience in tears, but this audience was far from the one she had known, both in temperament and location. If her spirit still watched over me, I knew it must be ashamed.

As I took my bow, with Saraki's hand in mine, I sought one last glimpse of my gentleman, but he had gone.

We left the stage as Granden, master of ceremonies and owner of the troupe, announced the next act, "The Beautiful Eila and her Trained Dogs." Sometimes I stayed to watch, but tonight I was tired and wanted out of my costume. Saraki lingered in the wings, begging a cigarette off of Granden.

"Terrible habit for a lady," he said, giving her a smoke and a sly wink.

I retreated to the dressing room, where a dim lamp illuminated chairs strewn with costumes and floorboards warping beneath the leaking roof. Polly was tugging suspenders over her slender shoulders. I yanked pins from my hair and pulled down my pompadour. My hair tumbled down my back, glossy black and shining in the low light.

"How's the crowd tonight?" Polly asked.

"Standard. There was a gentleman in a top hat, but he left already."

"Must have been Jon Albrook himself, if you found him worth noting," Polly said, bringing up one of the most eligible young bachelors in all of Lorinar, or so the papers claimed.

I made a face. "Hardly. I don't care for Jon Albrook, with those huge eyebrows."

"No one's ever good enough for you." Polly laughed.

"Just because I don't flirt with stagehands! But this gentleman *was* handsome, I'll give him that, and he's got money, by the looks of him. He'd be worth a second glance."

Someone knocked on the door. Polly went to open it. I knew it wasn't Granden. He never knocked; he'd just shout at us to open up.

Polly flung the door open wide. "Is this your handsome gentleman, Nim?"

Heat prickled my cheeks as my "handsome gentleman" saw me gaping like a fool, my hair undone and sash spilled around my feet, and a girl in suspenders giving me a tactless introduction, at that! I shot a venomous look at Polly.

He took off his hat—I hoped he meant to be polite, but then I realized it wouldn't have passed through the doorway. "I beg pardon," he said, his accent as crisp as his appearance. Now I could see the whole of him, the traveler's cape, the silk necktie, the dove-gray spats, and most striking of all, the pointed cuffs of his jacket that marked him as not just a gentleman, but a sorcerer. His smooth cheeks and forehead suggested a younger man than I had first assumed, no more than twenty—but his eyes seemed as old as the onyx they resembled, and all the more striking for the pale face that framed them.

I quickly gathered my wits. "What is it you want, sir?"

"May I speak with you a moment?"

"Of course." I snatched up a few of the pins I had dropped, twisting my hair into a loose bun.

"It's a simple matter, really," he continued, stepping into the room. Polly lingered by the door, obviously torn between curiosity and manners. "I'm looking for a singer."

"What sort of singer?" I mustn't trust him just because he was handsome. I knew how the men of Lorinar thought, what they wanted. To him, I was dark and foreign and crude.

His eyelids lowered slightly, and I felt he was carefully appraising me. "I'm looking for someone to accompany a musical automaton."

"An . . . an automaton, sir?"

He nodded. "A life-size automaton. It plays the piano, and I'd like to hire a singer as accompaniment. I think the contrast between living girl and lifelike machine would be striking."

"And you want *Nimira*?" Polly asked, voicing my own disbelief, although I would've much rather voiced it myself. In more delicate tones.

Granden stormed in just then, striking the door with his walking stick. "What's going on here? Who are you, sir? Bothering my girls? Polly, what the devil are you doing back here, you're almost up!"

"I am here on business," the man said. "Are you her employer?"

"I am indeed, sir!" Granden straightened himself and twisted the end of his mustache between two fingers. "Arnad Granden, at your service."

"My name is Hollin Parry. I'm inquiring after your singer."

Granden paused. He stepped toward me, putting a possessive arm around my shoulders. "Inquiring . . . after my Nimira? On what terms?"

"On terms the lady and I shall discuss, if she is willing." Mr. Parry reached inside an inner pocket of his jacket and handed me a card. "I am staying at the Royale, just across the river. You know it, I'm sure?"

Only as one of the finest hotels in the city of New Sweeling! I nodded, taking the card in a numb hand.

"I'll be there through tomorrow. Good evening to you." He bowed his head to me, stepped through the doorway, and replaced his hat.

"Good lord!" Granden shrieked, his voice a note higher than usual, and I prayed Mr. Parry couldn't hear him as he retreated. "Good lord! Hollin Parry, in the flesh—skulking around my girls!"

"You know him?"

"Well, you're not going with the likes of him," Granden continued. "Ridiculous."

"And why not? Who is he?" I tucked his calling card inside my corset.

"Don't you know what they say about him?"

I wished I did, so I wouldn't have to ask, but alas. "No."

"His wife died within a year of their wedding. They say her ghost now haunts his place. Makes you wonder what happened to her, eh?" Granden leaned close to me, his hot breath falling on my ear. When I tried to move away, he slammed his palm into the wall, blocking me. "You're not thinking of taking him up on his offer, are you?"

"I—I don't know. That's my business, not yours."

"I'll be damned."

"Get away from me. I want to change out of this stuff." I gave him a push to the door. You had to be firm with Granden. His eyes lingered on me as he left the room without a word.

I pulled out the calling card again. *A. Hollin Parry the Third*, it read, in fancy script. Of all the girls in the world, he'd chosen me. But to sing with an automaton? I'd seen a clockwork woman displayed at the fair, who'd moved her hands and face and eyes and even said "Hello," in a squeaky voice that gave me chills.

Of course the best singers in Lorinar wouldn't do. Mr. Parry likely thought to pair novelty with novelty. An automaton, a trouser girl: we were two of a kind to him—one a machine and the other somewhat less than human. I shouldn't think too much of it.

Still, he had called me "the lady," and he had sounded quite serious. I paid no mind to Granden's silly tales of ghosts. He wanted only to frighten me. Maybe with Mr. Parry, I'd have a better wage and something to eat besides brown bread and vegetables with the flavor boiled out. It might not be the glory of Tiansher's royal stage, but it had to be a step up from this place.

2

That night, back in the bedroom I shared with Saraki, I took out my good dress, a drab plaid with small, sharply puffed sleeves and a draped skirt. It had never been very pretty, but it was also out of fashion. I cringed to think of wearing it to the Royale, but I hadn't the money for something better.

Hard to believe, times like this, I had once had my pick of clothes: embroidered silk tunics the colors of saffron and jade, red sashes, dainty dancing slippers and sturdy walking shoes. I had bangles, beads, and headdresses for feasts and festivals; ribbons for my braids at school; and a quilted coat for cold days. That was before my family lost favor, before Mother's death, before Father became the subject of every wagging tongue with his debts and affairs. He sold the bangles and embroidery and slippers, and we moved north, to Uncle Sancham's farm. The quilted coat frayed at the elbows, and my feet had grown right out of the walking shoes.

When I left Tiansher—the true name of my country, not *Tassim*—I had saved just one ensemble: Mother's sky blue bird dancing costume and her embroidered wedding shoes. I had hidden them from Father when he sold our things. I still kept them, packed away in the valise at the foot of my bed.

Now I threw the plaid dress over a chair and slipped into my ratty nightgown. My bed creaked under my weight. A dozen painted birds looked down on me from the wall, plates torn from a book, while Saraki had arrayed her side of the room with calendars of comely girls and a yellowing poster for *Only a Maid*, starring Ethine May, Saraki's favorite.

Saraki did not come to the room. This was not unusual. She often spent the night with Granden. I shuddered to think of her lying with him, but she cooed over him like he was a wet puppy: "Poor thing, poor little thing." Granden attracted a certain sort of woman, for reasons I never quite understood.

One of Eila's dogs started barking, rousing all the others to join in, and Polly shouted for them to shut up. I closed my eyes. I yearned to break free of this place, so distant from the serene rooms and lush gardens of my childhood.

Yet, a part of me wished the decision was harder, that the troupe meant more to me—or perhaps, most of all, that I meant more to them. No one was sitting up with me, helping me decide, telling me not to go because they'd miss me. I had tried to make friends, I had *tried*—I'd just never been good at it.

To entrust my fate to a gentleman brought risk. If a trouser girl went missing, no one would care. If a trouser girl cried for help from inside a gentleman's carriage, no one would listen.

No, no—I mustn't think this way. Granden *would* try to scare me into staying. Before Jane left the troupe to marry, he'd told her no man would marry a girl with a baby, a dancing girl from a show. Jane believed in love, and I only had to believe in business. If Mr. Parry paid even half again what I made with Granden, I could start putting some away and send a token home to prove I'd done well after all.

In the morning, I woke early and packed a few treasured books and the remainder of my scant wardrobe into my valise on top of Mother's clothes and wedding slippers. I prayed, all the while, that I would safely unpack them in a new place. I left my stage costumes, assuming Mr. Parry would have his own ideas for my wardrobe in his show.

As the stairs creaked under my button-up shoes, Granden's door opened. He rushed to the top of the stairs and clutched the rail. "Nimira!"

Foiled. Well, perhaps if I didn't make a fuss, I could still slip out without incident.

"Good morning, Granden." I nodded back at him and kept walking.

Granden had gone drinking after the show, as usual. He staggered down after me, clutching his head. His mustache drooped. Gray chest hairs popped out of the collar of his nightshirt. "Look at you! All prettied up. Are you going to meet *Parry*?" He sneered the name.

"Yes." I tried to keep my voice calm, even as he veered close.

He made a grab for my hand. "I gave you those gloves."

"You did not." I yanked back. "I bought them myself."

He seized my shoulders. He wasn't tall, and dancing kept me strong and lithe, but he still had a man's strength, and I had a woman's clothes to hinder me. Hardly a fair contest.

His thin hands slipped to my arms. He tugged me close to him. His breath was rank—I hated few smells so much as last night's alcohol on a man's breath. "Haven't I been good to you, Nimira? I've never demanded anything."

"I sing and dance. You pay me. Of course you haven't demanded anything. There's nothing to demand." I had trouble sounding forceful with him breathing on me.

He pressed me against the door. "Damned if I'll let you go running off now."

"Let go of me!"

Saraki and Polly stood at the top of the stairs now, Polly in a man's nightshirt and Saraki in her corset and stockings. "What's going on?" Saraki rubbed her eyes.

Granden turned, and I took the moment to shove him off me. I clambered for the doorknob. Granden grabbed my sleeve and yanked. The seam tore with a terrific rip.

"Lay off her!" Polly shouted, coming down the stairs. Polly was thin as a lamppost but a hair taller than him and tough when she felt like it.

I threw open the door and ran, past the postman with his bag of letters and the ragman making his rounds. Morning fog shrouded the way ahead. I narrowly missed being run down by a horse crossing Broad Street.

Only when my lungs strained against my stays and my head spun did I stop at the square, gasping. Granden hadn't put up a chase. I inspected my torn sleeve for the first time, trying to tug it back into place. I couldn't disguise the gap, bridged only by a few feeble threads.

Not only must I go to the Royale in an old dress and hat, but they'd think I didn't even know how to keep my wardrobe tidy.

Granden had this parting shot, but I'd have the last laugh when I worked for a gentleman!

I didn't dare consider what I'd do if Mr. Parry had changed his mind.

A fearsome statue of a lady bearing a sword guarded the square, where the market sellers were putting up umbrellas and stacking apples and other fruits, some I still had yet to try since arriving on these shores. They smelled sweet and fresh now; as the sun peaked, the aroma would turn cloying. Already, the women came, some chattering rapidly, gossiping in clusters, hands waving for emphasis, others scolding the children who played at their feet. Many wore dark shawls around their heads, no matter the weather. They carried their babies on their backs. A barefoot little girl offered me a flower, just two cents, and I had to shake my head no.

As the towers of the Royale rose into view, so did my doubts. Would they even let me in, looking as I did? I crossed a bridge, an elegant span of arches and white stone. Gentlemen in tall hats and striped waistcoats flicked their eyes to me and away, as if to say, "What foul wind carried over this piece of trash?"

From a distance, I watched the doorman in his sharp uniform standing outside of the Royale, opening the door now for a pair of ladies in fine hats decorated with giant false roses. They spread their parasols as they came down the steps and circled around the fountain. I didn't usually envy the frippery of Lorinar's wealthy, but for a moment, how I yearned for a fine hat and parasol.

"She said it would be no trouble, but that was before she saw the place!" one exclaimed, laughing. They passed me by without notice.

I began the long march to the hotel steps, stopping to peer at my wavering reflection in the fountain pool. My old black feathered hat perched on my head like a dead crow. I heard mockery even in the genteel sound of steadily falling water.

Really, I needed only a big smudge of dirt on my cheek to complete the image.

The doorman regarded my approach with slightly pursed lips. "*May* I *help* you?" He almost shouted, enunciating each word.

"Yes, sir. I'm here to see Mr. Parry." I held up the card.

He looked surprised I could even speak the language but quickly recovered. "We do have a dress code at the Royale." He hesitated. "Wait here a moment, girl. I hope you're telling the truth or I'm sure Mr. Parry will not be pleased."

I waited as he ducked inside. The hour chimed nine, the bells of Lorinar's cathedrals ringing through the air. I wondered if Mr. Parry was even awake. Gentlemen kept late schedules sometimes, so I heard.

The doorman stepped out again, followed closely by another man, dark and severe from his mustache to his shining shoes. He gave me only the briefest glance. "I don't know what you think you're up to, girlie, but I must laugh to think of you setting foot in the Royale." He said this, of course, without anything resembling a laugh.

I hardly knew how to respond, with my worst fears unfolding before my eyes. I knew I hadn't dreamed my encounter with Mr. Parry, but how could I convince them? "Please, sir, Mr. Parry asked me to come here. I don't know what else to do."

"Look, I'm not sure what went on with you and Mr. Parry; it's not my business. But I am quite sure"—he spoke so precisely that his white teeth flashed at me—"that he would not ask a girl of your sort to come *here*. If you don't leave these steps right this moment, I will summon the police."

Shame filled my cheeks with heat, but I couldn't give up yet. "If you'd only let Mr. Parry know I'm here, he'll tell you!" I cried. "I'm no liar!"

My words bounced off unsympathetic faces. I couldn't bear my own reflection in their eyes: a girl dirty and disheveled, shouting nonsense. They thought I was a fallen woman.

The doorman tried to grab me then, but I ducked from his grasp. If I had to go, I'd let my own feet carry me, not be hauled off like an unruly drunk outside the pub. I had not taken two steps when I heard my savior speak.

"I'm told someone's asking for me?" Hollin Parry appeared through the hotel doors. He was hatless today, in an ordinary short sack coat, and he looked expectant. My knees fairly buckled with relief.

"No, sir," the severe man said. "It's no one. We're taking care of it."

"Miss Nimira," Mr. Parry said, eyes roving to my torn sleeve. "What on earth happened?"

When he said my name, the doorman and the severe gentleman took their notice of me so fast it was almost comical.

I forced a bright smile. "Good morning, Mr. Parry, I'm fine. It's only that these gentleman didn't believe the legitimacy of your card." I flashed it through the air.

"Oh, no, no," the severe man said. "It isn't that, not at all; I didn't see the card—"

Mr. Parry held up a hand, his demeanor icy. "I understand all too well. It's lucky for you that some young lad on your staff saw fit to inform me; I shall certainly tip him accordingly." He nodded at me. "Well, come on up to my suite and we'll discuss terms."

Mr. Parry strolled through the lobby without a hint of shame at my company, although I knew very well that my torn plaid dress and horrid hat didn't belong between the lush carpets and the ornate gasolier. In the corner, a man played a slow, gentle tune on a grand piano. Stubby palms surrounded overstuffed furniture trimmed in fringe that hid the feet. Bouquets of pink and white flowers perfumed the air.

We stepped into an elevator—I knew of them but had never ridden inside one. It reminded me of a gilded birdcage. A uniformed attendant stood within. To his credit, he didn't blink at my appearance as he shut the doors on us. "Top floor, sir?"

"Yes."

The attendant operated a handle, sending us climbing. I counted the floors as we passed. It helped distract me from the unsettling sensation that the elevator pulleys could snap loose and plunge us to the ground. We came to a stop at the seventh floor, and the attendant opened the doors. "Watch your step, sir. Miss."

Mr. Parry opened the door to his penthouse suite and gestured to a chair upholstered in ivory damask. My dress rustled against it. A fire crackled gently in the hearth. The room smelled of breakfast, and I tried to ignore my own hunger and look at ease. Mr. Parry sat down across from me and draped one leg over the other.

"Miss Nimira." His gaze was even. He didn't blink much. "Now tell me. What happened outside? I'll lodge a complaint."

"Nothing happened."

"They tore your dress." He tweaked the injured fabric with thumb and finger.

"No, sir. It's nothing." It pained me to dwell on the subject. Even though Mr. Parry had defended me, the memory still jabbed at my pride. "I'm fine, I assure you. Please, I'd like to hear about the job."

He smiled as if something I'd said had satisfied him. "I came into possession of this automaton some months ago, and I knew immediately that I wished to display it. It's said to be fairy-made, the finest piece of clockwork you'll ever see. It plays a number of popular tunes, older ones, the sort that could draw a broad crowd. But I thought it really should have a singer. I've gone through a few girls already, lovely girls with lovely voices, but none lasted past the second practice session." He paused, his expression unreadable. "You see, they claim it's haunted."

My brows lifted. "Haunted?"

He smirked. "They've said that it moans, or turns its eyes to look at them. I've never seen it do anything out of the ordinary. I think they're only imagining things. Even so, I'm looking for a girl who isn't afraid of a ghost."

I couldn't decide how I felt about ghosts. Every summer back home, when the court traveled to Shala, all of us children had played around the cave mouth where people said ghosts lived, scaring ourselves silly. I'd usually been the one shouting, "There isn't any such thing!" when the other girls shrieked that they'd seen a *face*. But the cave ghosts of old stories were one thing, haunted automatons another.

"It's fairy-made?" I asked. Tiansher had no fairies, and I didn't understand the repulsion and fascination they held for the people of Lorinar. Fairies occupied almost half the continent, from the Western Wall to the western sea. In stories they were often lovely tricksters, casting spells and glamours to lure humans or steal from them, but in the few photographs I'd seen, they looked no different from humans to me, disappointingly so.

"Supposedly, but I wouldn't be concerned. I'm a sorcerer myself, and if I suspected it was dangerous, I'd certainly do something about it. There's just something uncanny about the thing, and that's what frightens the girls off, I believe." He shrugged a little.

"Well . . . I don't think I'm afraid of ghosts."

"I have my hopes for you, Miss Nimira. I've been investigating all the singers in the city, looking for just the right girl."

"And you think I'm the right girl?" Even though he had given me his card and invited me to his rooms, I still couldn't believe a man of Lorinar had seen my potential despite the trousers and the cheap sets.

"Yes, you had such a look of defiance there on the stage. Like you thought the whole thing beneath you. I somehow don't think you'd come to me screaming and carrying on about ghosts."

Now genuine embarrassment swept my face. Goodness, he knew just what I was thinking when I performed.

"Besides that, your voice has range and passion."

Passion. Mother had repeated to me, time and time again, that while dancing was the highest expression of a woman's physical beauty and grace, singing was the highest expression of her passion and depth of feeling. Sometimes I forgot I was an artist when my grace and passion went forever unappreciated, but Mr. Parry had seen it. Perhaps my efforts had not been in vain.

"I hope you'll accept," Mr. Parry said.

"I accept most humbly and gratefully, sir. I only hope I won't disappoint you."

"You won't," he said, and in those simple words, he gave me the one thing I wanted more than money: the acknowledgment that when he looked at me, he saw more than a trouser girl worth two cents' admission.

3

Over the rattling of the coach wheels, I still heard the shouts of merchants, the pleas of beggars, the distant clang of a blacksmith's hammer, and the horn of a river barge. I hoped my new home would bring the peace of gardens, starry skies, and shady forests. I might never have come to Lorinar if someone had told me the city had hardly a tree or flower, and that columns spouting smoke would be the view from my window.

Mr. Parry sat across from me, hands folded. He had a knack for not exactly looking at me, yet not exactly looking away from me. The subtle, masculine scent of his cologne drifted my way.

I clutched my gloves in my lap. *Please let this be the right decision.* I tried to tell myself I trusted Mr. Parry, but I wondered if his good looks hadn't dulled my judgment. Now that I had committed myself, Granden's warnings spiraled out of control. A ghost might wander the halls, white skin drawn across her bones. At night she would hover around my bed, clawing at my covers in a cold room, crying for revenge. A clockwork man with mechanical movements and glittering human eyes would play the piano on and on without ever tiring.

Mr. Parry glanced at me with eyebrows gently raised. I hoped sorcerers couldn't read minds.

"I wonder what you're thinking of," he said. "Something not quite pleasant, if the wrinkle of your brow is any indication."

"Oh . . ." I waved my hand. "Nothing."

"How long have you lived in Lorinar?" he asked. "You speak almost like a native."

"Three years. I came when I was near fourteen. I already knew some of the language. My teacher used to say I was good with languages." It seemed so long ago that I had ever had a teacher, that I had ever been concerned only with education and not survival.

"They teach their girls in Tassim?"

"Some do." I hoped he didn't frown upon my education, as many men would. My father's father had insisted on education for high-born girls. He'd died before I was born, but I'd attended the same school as my aunt Vinya before me, learning reading, writing, history, and languages, along with my mother's instruction in traditional song and dance.

"It's wise, I think. No one wants a silly wife."

"No, you certainly wouldn't call my mother a silly wife." Indeed, my mother would have had the perfect retort to such a remark.

As the carriage broke free of the city crowds, its pace quickened. The jerking and rocking knocked my teeth together. Fences of stone and wood reined in sheep, cows, and rows of fruit trees and vegetables growing in the late springtime sun. Vines crawled up the chimneys of old stone farmhouses, while the newer wooden homes had broad, inviting porches. Sometimes I saw children playing in yards or women marching on the roadside, carrying pails of berries, baskets of eggs. I had not seen such things in years. My heart wanted to fly from the carriage—to feel the grass tickle my legs as the fresh scent of it tickled my nose.

Mr. Parry's voice startled me from my reverie. "Your eyes are wide. I suppose you have not been to the country in some time?"

"No..."

He smiled. "I hope you will enjoy the gardens at Vestenveld."

"Vestenveld?"

"My estate."

"Oh, I'm sure I will. I love gardens; I miss them. The court palaces of Tiansher have beautiful gardens." I hoped I sounded worldly. I wanted him to know I had once dwelt in my country's finest hall, that my mind and manners bore no resemblance to my shabby clothes.

"You have seen the court palace? Tell me of it," he said. "It shall make the trip go faster."

"I lived in the court palace," I said. "When I was a little girl. Lots of people live there. It's like a city in itself."

"So, you are a maiden of the court? That explains your regal air."

I was very pleased—I had kept my regal air, then. "Yes, sir."

"Are your parents of royal blood, then?"

"My father was ... I'm not sure what the term would be here. A ... lord?"

"How about your mother?"

"My mother danced and sang in the royal troupe. The artists in the troupe are very highly regarded." I knew he'd be unlikely to think well of her, no matter how I explained her role. People in

Lorinar didn't seem to treat performers, even the best of them, with the same reverence I had known back home. I had been shocked to hear that some people refused to attend the theater on religious grounds.

But if he had a disparaging thought toward her, he left it unvoiced. "And how, may I ask, did the daughter of such esteemed individuals end up in a cheap show in New Sweeling?"

I should have seen the conversation taking this unfortunate direction and steered it elsewhere. "My mother died and my father—well, he fell out of favor. Favor is very fickle at court, of course." Not that Father hadn't deserved it—his affair with Lady Ajira, begun before Mother was even cold in her grave, had been the scandal of the year, and money had flowed from the family coffers to the pot in the center of a card table until he couldn't go anywhere for fear of running into someone he owed money. "We left to live with my uncle. I came here to seek my fortune."

"And I take it you're still seeking?"

I turned to the window, shamed by my failure. Everything had unraveled since Mother died.

"Perhaps you'll find what you seek at Vestenveld," Mr. Parry said, before he, too, turned to the window.

Delayed by spring showers, we reached the town of Pelswater in the twilight. The rains had slowed to a mist, and through this I saw the dim, wavering light of streetlamps. Shops had shut their doors for the night, and lights shone from the upper-story apartments. The taverns remained open. I heard the faint tune of a fiddle drift on the night air. A few rather haggard-looking men stood on corners or roamed the rain-slick streets.

Mr. Parry's estate lay just outside of town. The carriage pulled down a winding road, leading toward a great manor, made doubly impressive by the reflection pool before it. Statues kept silent watch over the water.

"Vestenveld," he said. "The Parry estate. How do you like it?" He watched me.

"Lovely," I said, although my first thought was what a cold and lonely face the house wore in the cloudy night. Lights glowed from just a scattered handful of windows, while the building itself looked endless, with arches and stone towers and dozens of separate roofs. The architect seemed to have tacked on majesty wherever he could find a spot.

"I hope you will be happy here." Mr. Parry gave me another reserved smile as the coach circled around the driveway to the front steps.

The rattling of the wheels and the clopping of horses' hooves halted. Mr. Parry helped me down from the coach. Insects chirped in the cool, rain-scented night. Two golden statues of tigers frozen midpounce guarded the front door.

"They're beautiful," I said as we passed them, running my hand along a perfectly formed paw, still slick from the rain. The sculptor had not missed a detail. From the pads of the paws to the little rounded ears, they looked just like the tigers in the menagerie at court. "So lifelike!"

"So they are," he said. "My father hunted tigers in Hangal. Some men prefer to make rugs of them, but my father was an alchemist, and he turned them to gold."

I jerked my hand back with sudden horror. "*Real* tigers?"

"It's no worse than a rug, is it?"

Slowly, I closed my mouth. True, we had fur rugs in Tiansher, too, but not with such expressions on their faces—suddenly, the tigers looked as much frightened as fierce.

The door creaked heavily on its hinges, opening to a vestibule. Gaslights dangled from the ceiling, softly illuminating two matched paintings, one of a man fighting a dragon and the other of him dying in a woman's arms, bleeding from his side. A busy pair of footsteps echoed from the hall, and a meaty-armed old woman in a dark gray dress emerged. "Good evening, sir."

"Miss Rashten?" He sounded less than pleased. "Where is the rest of my staff?"

"You know I like to see what sort of guests you bring around," she said as Mr. Parry reluctantly allowed her to take his hat and gloves.

"Well, this is Miss Nimira. She is a singer from New Sweeling."

"Ah. Miss Nimira." Miss Rashten gave me a curt smile from a wrinkled face framed by curls and a ruffled cap, the sort I saw in older books. Her eyes flicked to my sleeve. "We should get you off to bed. You look spent."

I didn't wish to be gotten off to anywhere by Miss Rashten. She wore a servant's uniform, but an ordinary servant would surely have received a reprimand for the impertinent comment about seeing what kind of guests Mr. Parry brought around.

We were coming forward into the main hall, a vast room where furniture jockeyed to fill space. The high ceiling, painted with dancing nymphs, drained the intimacy from our voices, leaving every word hollow. In the grand dwellings of Tiansher, empty space was meant to encourage serenity, but this vastness seemed cold and forbidding.

"Are you hungry, Miss Nimira?" Mr. Parry asked.

"Yes, sir."

"Miss Rashten, would you mind telling the kitchen to send some supper to her room? We'll be along in a moment." He dismissed her with a nod, to my relief.

We stood alone in the midst of thronelike chairs of dark wood and tables topped with vases. I had the sense that the chairs were never sat in and the tables never used.

"My father had the house expanded when I was a boy," Mr. Parry said. "We're in the oldest part now. It's not the height of style these days."

"Oh, that's all right. I surely don't know what the height of style looks like."

Mr. Parry waved me on toward the stair. "The servants live in the east wing. Your quarters will be in the west wing, on the second floor. The upper stories are closed off, since my father died, but you're free to explore the rest of the house. Can you read, Miss Nimira?"

"Oh, yes. I love to read."

"I have an extensive library, and you're welcome to it."

Upstairs, Mr. Parry led me down a carpeted corridor. I wondered if it was exactly proper, him showing me to my bedroom without a chaperone. Of course, we'd already been alone in his suite at the Royale, so I supposed this was no different.

He opened a door. "This is your room."

As if by magic, a bowl of stew already rested on the table in the center of the room, letting off curls of steam, with bread and milk beside, and lit candles. This part of the house didn't seem to have gaslights. A gentle fire crackled in the hearth. Fresh flowers spread from a vase set before a large mirror, and by the window sat a pillow-heaped chair, its frame woven like a basket. A perfect spot to read.

"My wife started refurnishing this room before she died," Mr. Parry said. "Her friends would stay here. The bedroom is through that door." He backed out of the doorway. "I'll leave you to your supper. Ring when you're ready to dress for bed." He pointed to the bell pull, a slender stick of metal with a handle, mounted to the wall.

"Thank you, sir. Very much."

He left the room, and I parted the curtains. My room over-looked a garden, but I could make out only vague shapes in the darkness. In the distance, a ridge of tall and narrow trees shook in the wind that followed the storm. The waning round moon cast enough cold light to see their dancing silhouettes. Nothing in the city ever looked like that. I clutched my hand to my breast. I could hardly believe I'd wake every morning to look upon trees once again.

The aroma of slow-cooked meat finally lured me from the window. I had almost forgotten how good food could be. We had cheap meat at Granden's if we had it at all, still tough after hours of boiling. I had learned to gnaw with determination at the gristle, for we were always hungry. Here, I even had butter for the bread. I hadn't had butter on my bread since the winter holidays.

Miss Rashten came and unbuttoned my dress. She said noth-ing as she looked me over. When our eyes met, she smiled in a way more amused than kind. Perhaps the long day had already jarred my nerves, but I had the sense that she was testing me, perhaps waiting for me to make some faux pas.

Still, as she whisked away the dress, I felt burdens sliding off me. It had been so long since anyone had brought me a meal or mended my clothes. I could put up with a few scrutinizing glances for the privilege of being taken care of. As a child, I had taken it for granted, but never again.

I pulled back the sheets and sank into a huge mattress, so far from the ground that I imagined the bed floating away as I dreamed. I was so used to a tiny room, hearing Eila's dogs and Polly's snoring through the walls, and Saraki's slow breath on the rare occasions she wasn't in Granden's rooms. I listened and heard nothing but the slow creaks of an old house turning in for the night.

I blew out the candle. Sleep crept in with the darkness.

4

In the morning, the servants filled a tub with hot water from brass canisters, and I had a bath—a real, true bath that left my fingers wrinkled. I lathered my long hair and scrubbed down my arms and legs with a fat bar of soap. The water turned gray. Baths had not come often enough at Granden's.

A young maid brought me fresh underclothes. I relished the soft, clean cotton of the chemise and pantalettes against my skin. I had stockings of silk now and an imported Verrougian corset in blue.

I was quite cheerful even as she whispered, "You're going to sing with the clockwork man, aren't you?"

"That's right." She called him "the clockwork man," I noted, although Mr. Parry had only ever said "automaton."

"You're brave, miss." She was combing out my hair.

"Is he *really* haunted?" With the sun spilling in my window, I didn't believe an automaton could scare me.

"Oh, I've heard him, miss! It's true what they've said; he moans and twitches. Like he was trying his best to speak to me. I nearly jumped out of my skin! Of course, I don't want to scare you off." She took a section of my hair and separated it; gentle tugs on my scalp signaled she had begun braiding. "Such pretty hair, miss."

"It's my one vanity," I said, although I actually had several vanities. It was never wise to admit that, however. In Tiansher, they said your lips would shrivel. "He truly moans and twitches?"

She nodded. "I s'pose I could have imagined it. Mr. Parry says he's sure I did, but if that's so, it *was* the realest imagining I ever had. I might be accused of daydreaming from time to time, but it stays in my head."

I smiled. "I'm not afraid of an automaton. Even if he does moan and twitch, I don't suppose that ever hurt anybody."

Nevertheless, I felt a twinge of apprehension as she showed me to the sunlit room where Mr. Parry awaited with an automaton as large as a man.

It sat still on a bench at a small pianoforte. Large brown eyes stared glassily ahead from a finely crafted face, its lips shut and perked in a smile. I nearly believed it could come to life with the slightest provocation. Soft brown hair framed its forehead and cheekbones, with delicate ears poking out, and the rest drawn back at his neck into a blue satin bow. Men didn't wear their hair that long anymore.

"It is an amazing piece, isn't it?" Mr. Parry lifted aside the back of the automaton's coat and began to wind him with a silver key. Even his clothes were works of art. His coat of deep green velvet was embroidered with red and black patterns that curled around the cuffs, the broad collar, and the back pleat. The buttons were of carved wood, just like the buckles on his shoes. *Fairy-tale shoes*, I thought, with their heels painted red. He wore knickers and silk stockings.

Through the chipping paint of the pianoforte, I could still make out birds, trees, and deer traipsing around the sides, while the legs had been carved in the shape of snakes.

"It's beautiful." Fascination replaced fear, and I ran my fingertip along the automaton's sleeve. The velvet was nearly as soft as a rabbit's fur, and beneath it I traced the line of a metallic skeleton. "I've never seen anything like it. The carving and needlework are . . . breathtaking." The embroidery stood up to anything I'd seen in Tiansher, and embroidery was a specialty of women of the court.

"The fairies do make beautiful things," Mr. Parry said. "They're tied to nature—they draw power from it; they die without access to it. Naturally, their art reflects the bond. The paintings on the pianoforte are a fine example, although they could use restoration. Here, he's wound—step back and watch."

I jumped as the automaton jerked to life with a muted but steady grinding sound.

His torso slowly moved back. His chest began to rise and fall with feigned breath, his hands parted, and his eyes moved from side to side, as if he surveyed the piano before him and would look up at any moment and see me standing there.

He began to play. His eyes darted left and right, watching his hands. His fingers moved up and down in precise motions, playing a sentimental standard I recognized: "In Springtime Blooms the Rose." His music bore an ethereal quality, as if it didn't quite belong in the real world, so pure and strange it was over the clicking of his mechanism.

Suddenly, his eyes lifted up and to the side, right at me.

I made a peep of surprise before the eyes lowered again. "Oh—he looked at me!"

"Yes, he always looks up a few times. Watch, he'll look ahead in a moment—there, see?" he scoffed. "It's only a machine."

"Of course, yes. It just surprised me, is all. He does look so very . . . not *real* . . . but *alive*."

"Only due to the skill of his builders. And my reputation as a sorcerer hasn't helped. People are far too eager to believe sorcerers enchant everything we touch, but good sorcerers know magic is dangerous."

"Oh, indeed." Sorcerers in Tiansher had always frightened me, from the mysterious shamans of court to the cackling charm-sellers of the villages.

In another moment, the automaton stopped playing. Once again, he surveyed the piano, peered out at the imaginary crowd, and then bent forward slightly, as if he could now relax.

A strange sadness came over me when the automaton's mechanism ground to a stop. The hairs on my arms lifted, and I forced back a shiver. What if he had looked at me? No, no, of course he hadn't, but . . . I understood why the other girls might have imagined things, faced with such a strange creation.

"The fairies made him . . . but he does not play fairy songs?" I asked Mr. Parry.

"At the auction, they said he was altered at some point to play songs from Lorinar. Do you know 'Fair She Was, Well He Loved Her'?"

"I think I know the melody . . . da da da, da da *da* da . . . ?"

"Yes, exactly."

". . . not the words, though."

He rummaged in a basket and plucked out a song sheet. "Can you try these if I wind him again?"

"Yes, sir."

Mr. Parry wound the automaton once more, and now he played the sweet strains of a Lorinarian love song. Even as I hummed along with the chorus, trying to find my way, I wondered what his original fairy melodies had sounded like. I'd heard many songs in my three years in Lorinar. Even on the ship over, a group of returning missionaries gathered after dinner and sang, when enough of them could hold down their dinners and stumble from their berths, that is.

Mr. Parry watched me, arms crossed, tapping his hand against his elbow in time.

I tried the first verse. *"Years ago, the stage was set . . ."*

He came to peer over my shoulder. "Close, but a little slower, a little softer . . . 'The stage was set' . . . like that." He finished the verse. His singing voice had a certain charming and unexpected frailty. When I joined in with him at the chorus, I worried he might stop, but he sang with me until the end.

Our voices silenced, and we heard the automaton grind to a stop behind us. Our eyes met over the lyric sheet. A smile played at Mr. Parry's lips.

"Well," he said. "It's been a long time since I've done anything like that."

"Singing? But it seems like everyone in Lorinar likes to sing! Even the fishmongers."

The tentative smile broke into a true one. "Is that your impression of our fair nation, then? It's no wonder they say abroad that we have no culture." He made an abrupt turn back to the basket of song sheets, and I had mere seconds for a thousand dreams to race through my mind, for . . .

I had brought a true smile to Mr. Parry's lips. No one needed to tell me that a smile didn't often form there.

He tucked more songs under his arm, wound the automaton, and guided me through the rest of the repertoire. Our eyes met more times than I could count. I saw more of his smiles: the sly grin, the amused twitch of his lips, the full-blown prelude to laughter that showed his straight teeth.

I hoped I pleased him. I didn't know what else to do but give smiles I hoped were winsome and try not to let my native accent creep in.

Had Mr. Parry hired me with an intent beyond singing? He treated me almost like a suitor might. A true gentleman suitor, with cautious tread and flashes of feeling. My future would be safe in a place like this.

How I craved safety.

When we finished singing, Mr. Parry offered up a second silver key. "One for you, Miss Nimira."

I took it in my palm, turning it over, this fairy thing. The top was shaped like a sprig of leaves. Mr. Parry's hand had warmed it.

"I want you to come and practice here whenever you like. I hope to show you off before long. Mr. Smollings has expressed interest in seeing the automaton when he next visits."

"Who's Mr. Smollings?"

"The ambassador of magic. Head of the Sorcerer's Council. An old friend of my father's."

"The ambassador of magic? Didn't something happen to him?" Although I didn't keep up with Lorinar's politics, even I hadn't missed the news this past spring, that the ambassador of magic had been found dead, thought to be murdered by fairy bandits who lingered near the wall separating the human and fairy lands.

"You're thinking of Garvin Pelerine. The previous ambassador. Mr. Smollings has taken his place." A brief furrow marred his forehead before he continued. "You can rest for today. I'm sure you'll want to explore the gardens and the house. The library will be of particular interest. It's the door past the west stair, in the hall."

"Thank you, sir."

"My pleasure—but before you lose yourself, I'll have lunch sent to your room. Exploring is better on a full stomach."

The same fair-haired young maid from breakfast brought a tray of food to my boudoir. She lifted the silver cover to reveal a spread of cold sliced pork, crusty bread, cucumbers, and pastry filled with the first peaches of the season. I didn't realize how hungry I was until the aroma hit my nose, and I heartily thanked her for bringing me such delights.

She bobbed a curtsy. "You're welcome, miss." She turned to go. I knew maids should do their work without complaint or conversation. How many times had I missed the loyal family servants since I'd come to Lorinar? Now it felt strange to be served by a nameless girl no older than myself.

"What's your name?" I called.

"Linza, miss." She gave me a shy smile. "Did you make it through your visit with the clockwork man all right?"

"No moaning or twitching," I said. I didn't tell her I had found him more intriguing than scary. She might think me odd.

She widened her eyes. "Wait and see, miss." Then she stepped back, bobbing her head at me as if apologizing for the remark, before she hurried off.

I wanted to ask Linza exactly what had happened with the

other girls Mr. Parry hired. Perhaps more than that, I wished to talk to another girl, my age, and feel the ease of friendship. Of course, Linza probably had silver to polish or floors to sweep, and Mr. Parry might frown on me becoming too familiar with the servants.

Well, if I couldn't expect friendship with Linza, I vowed to be kind to her at least. I wouldn't need company here, at any rate, not with a library and gardens to roam!

I ate the pork a little too fast to be ladylike, and my racing hunger slowed. I could already tell I'd regret stuffing myself. I flopped back in my chair with a sigh.

Outside, wind tossed the frail trees about. The skies promised more rain. The garden walk would have to wait.

I gathered my dishes back onto the tray and covered them with the lid, leaving them as tidy as possible for Linza, then set off to explore the house. I headed for the library, poking in rooms on the way, and now I could finally see what I had only glimpsed before: the billiard room, linked to the smoking room, both with their masculine airs, heavy furnishings, and Hangalian carpets. The drawing room had grown quite dusty, like Mr. Parry did not employ enough help to keep up, or perhaps he only needed a wife to manage things.

The library, however, did not disappoint. A statue of a woman with a scroll tucked under her arm and a torch in her raised hand guarded the room; I imagined her as some goddess of wisdom. Books stretched so far above my head that rolling ladders clung to the shelves to access them. In the room's center, chairs and tables clustered.

Miss Rashten found me in one of the chairs hours later, buried deep in a tale of swashbuckling, revolution, and ripped bodices, while outside the rain poured down.

"You'll ruin your eyes, you know," she said. "Why don't you turn on a lamp?" I'd hardly noticed. But now that she mentioned it, I realized I was holding the book to my nose in the dim. She continued. "Mr. Parry would like to meet you for dinner in the tower, so we'd best get you into something suitable."

"In the tower?"

"Mr. Parry has taken his meals there since the mistress died."

Miss Rashten kept her eyes locked on me until I shut the book. I noted my page and started to follow her. "Where is Linza?"

"Linza is otherwise occupied. I'm attending you this evening, Miss Nimira. I want to get some idea of your character."

"Oh." It sounded almost like a threat.

We reached my quarters, and even as she pinned up the hem of the dress, she prickled me with words. "I'm not sure what the master is thinking, putting you in pink—pink does not do with skin like yours."

I joined Mr. Parry in the tower—not the top of the tower, which must have been shut off like the rest of the upper stories, but the second floor, a small circular room with three huge windows overlooking the woods. A table already bore a spread of food: thin soup, more crusty bread, and some kind of drink in a silver pitcher. A footman waited in the shadows, in the invisible way of servants. Mr. Parry was standing, waiting for me to arrive before he took his seat. The footman pulled out a chair for me.

I smoothed my skirts underneath me and took the heavy, carved chair.

"A pity it rains," Mr. Parry said, pouring himself the drink: something red and bubbly. "I suppose the gardens had to wait."

He held the pitcher over my glass and I nodded. "Yes, sir. I don't mind. I explored the house, the library—I spent ages reading." I felt

I was reciting a script. "The sun might have set without my notice."
I hoped I was making proper conversation. I'd never shared a table
with a gentleman before, unless you counted the days when I was a
wee thing on my mother's lap.

I lifted my glass. The drink tasted of cherries and spice and
sparkled in my nose.

"So, you've been enjoying the house? It needs new furniture in
nearly every room, but when my wife died . . ."

"So young," I said, searching for the appropriate words for such
a tragic circumstance. Granden's warning flitted across my mind,
but Hollin looked too sad to be a murderer . . . didn't he?

"The sickness struck her very fast. Very like the same sickness
that took my mother to an early grave." He forced a weak smile.
"The Parry family doesn't have the best luck, I suppose."

"It could happen to anyone." I was tempted to burden him
with tales of my own family, but even men who liked educated
women didn't like to hear them complain. "Were you close to your
mother?"

"Mother and my uncle Simalt. Father's older brother. He was an
art collector who traveled the world, more lighthearted than my
father. I think my mother wished she'd married the other Parry, and
I wanted to grow up to be him." He managed a smile. "Father was
never too happy about that. But I suppose it doesn't matter. They're
all gone now." He shrugged. "And you, Nimira? You came to Lorinar
alone, didn't you?"

"Yes, sir."

"Do you still write home?"

The first footman took our soup bowls away while another
brought the main course; chicken swimming in a golden sauce
with prunes. I poked one with my fork. "No. The letters travel so

slowly." I had meant to write home as soon as I had good news. I supposed I finally had good news, but would it count after four years of silence? Home felt distant as a dream, and I didn't like to speak of it. I yearned to see the mist shrouding the Shai mountains, to taste the juicy yellow flesh of mangos, to smell the toasting spices that anticipated a delicious meal. I missed the pageantry of court, the swirling colors of the dancer's costumes, and the way everyone said I took after my mother. No one in Lorinar would ever know my mother.

You must be Mamira's daughter. Visitors to court would know me without introduction, having seen my mother dance, we looked so alike.

"Would you go home now if you could?" Mr. Parry asked.

"Sometimes I consider it. To marry, that is." I wasn't sure I should talk to him about marriage. "Though if I went home to marry, I'd probably end up a farmer's wife, and I'd rather have my freedom and my art ... even if it means living on pennies."

"Is it such a terrible fate, marrying a farmer?"

"Oh, not for some. I just wasn't raised to it. And it really is a dirty business, tending goats and scrubbing laundry in rivers and all that sort of thing."

"You must be very committed to your art, to give up your homeland to pursue it."

"Nothing else makes me so happy."

"Even that disgraceful show you were in? How did you end up working there?"

"It's hard to find work anymore, sir. Back home, I'd heard that trouser girls made a great deal of money here, but when I got off the boat, everyone said that day has passed."

He nodded a little. "True. Like everything else, what the rich liked yesterday is what the poor will like tomorrow." Mr. Parry's eyes gleamed in the soft light. "I see a similarity between us, Nimira. We've each been thwarted from the life we should have been born to. Is it too late for us, then?"

"I don't know, sir." I hoped it wasn't too late for me, of course, but I didn't understand exactly what he meant.

"Maybe it isn't." The gleam in his eyes blossomed to a spark.

My heart pounded.

He lowered his eyes and pulled bits of meat from the bone with his fork. "The rain is slowing. Tomorrow might be sunny yet."

I let my breath go. Not yet.

5

The next morning, I skipped my usual routine of stretching and dance exercises, with apologies to my mother. I was anxious to look upon the automaton again, but I sat patiently while Linza helped me into a day dress of striped white and blue taffeta and then dressed my hair.

I didn't quite understand why I was drawn to the automaton; perhaps it was simply the beauty of his clothes and the piano, or perhaps it was the whisper of fairy magic that clung to him. I only knew that I itched to try winding him with my own hand.

The curtains stood open behind him. The morning sun lent a warm light to his frozen form, bringing out the colors of his clothing. My key would release him. I would let him play.

His clothes concealed the winding mechanism—his vest had a full front, but no back. Pins secured it to a shirt of fine white linen, which had an open slit down the back from neck to waist, displaying the clockwork man's innards. I could see the heart of him, a golden drum stacked with rings of metal, each cut with grooves. Surrounding the drum was a tangle of thin metal rods, tiny jointed pieces, and wheels and gears, some silver and some with a duller, brassy sheen, all constructed with great delicacy. Although I knew nothing of the workings of automatons, I had never seen a machine that came so close to art, and I started to run my fingers along the metal parts, only to snatch my hand away in surprise; I had not expected them to feel warm.

I recalled Linza's warning: *Wait and see.*

In the center of his back was a small golden plate from which the keyhole beckoned between two screws. The plate was stamped with a few lines of tiny letters, in a script I couldn't read—the maker's mark, I guessed.

I slid the key into the hole with a satisfying click.

It almost seemed to turn itself. I needed only give the gentlest nudge for it to make a revolution at first, but it grew more taut as I went, and finally it wouldn't budge. I pulled the key out and stepped back, reaching for the song sheets as he ground to life.

I riffled through them, waiting to hear a note.

No note came.

I looked up. The automaton's hands waved back and forth over the pianoforte but didn't touch a key.

Was he broken? Had I broken him? My heart scurried to a faster rhythm. I came around to see him from the front. His eyes swung up to meet mine, and they stayed there for a long moment. I didn't move. Not the slightest breath left me.

His eyes lowered to the keys. His hands jerked, as if they fought to defy their nature. They began to play, slowly and deliberately, a simple tune that sounded more and more familiar as it went. A child's song I'd heard sung in the streets of Lorinar . . .

"The alphabet?" I whispered. "I don't remember you playing that..."

He stopped halfway through the melody. His eyes rose again.

"Mmm." A grunt came from his throat, while his mouth stayed shut in a closed-lip smile.

I shrieked, colliding with a table as I stepped back. His eyes followed me. He *was* haunted. All the other girls had been right!

My lips trembled so badly I could hardly speak. "Y—you spoke!"

"Mmm."

Now my hands trembled, too. All of me trembled. I went to the door.

All the other girls...

And Mr. Parry had sent them away. He hadn't believed any of them. He wouldn't believe me. The automaton must have never come alive for him.

I had even said to Mr. Parry and Linza both that an automaton couldn't hurt me. Of course, this was before I saw the thing jerk his hands around, before I had heard the anxious grunt escape those sealed lips.

The automaton was silent now. He sat erect, eyes swiveled toward me, hands fixed over the keys. His mechanism still clicked, and he should have *had* to play, but he didn't.

I took a deep breath and held my hands tight behind me.

I *had* to bite back my fear and keep this quiet from Mr. Parry. He'd send me away like the rest. I'd have to start over again. I'd have nothing.

An automaton couldn't hurt me, after all. Could he? I smoothed my hands over my skirt again and again, trying to stop their shaking. Oh, heaven protect me.

"Are you trying to talk to me?" I said in a whisper. My voice wouldn't go any louder if I wished it.

"Mmm."

"But . . . you can't speak?"

"Mmm." He began to play the tune again, and he kept grunting, sounding urgent.

He was responding to my questions. There really was something intelligent peering out at me from those eyes.

"You're trying to tell me you want to communicate through the piano?"

"Mmm."

I thought for a moment "You want to play the letters of the alphabet?"

"Mmm." He touched the piano key farthest to the left and hummed the note that matched A. Then he moved to the next, touched the key, and hummed the note for B.

I nodded in understanding, although my anxious head bobbed so fast I must have looked like a marionette. "You mean to press the first key for A, and the next key for B, and so on?"

"Mmm, mmm!"

"I—I'll need some paper. Can you wait here?"

"Mmm."

I left the room and started to dash down the hall, but then forced my steps to slow. I must not show my fear or my surprise to anyone else in the house. I didn't want Mr. Parry to think I was just another silly girl running from the automaton he didn't believe was haunted.

I wondered what he wanted to tell me.

The library would surely have pen and paper, but I hoped to

find some tucked away without encountering Mr. Parry. I passed my bedroom, and another bedroom, somber and dusty, before coming upon a small study. Just the thing I needed, yet I had a certain reluctance to enter the room.

Taxidermy lined the walls—the heads of boar, gazelle, leopard—even a unicorn. Bad luck to kill unicorns, at least we thought so back home, although this one wasn't pretty like the unicorns in books. It was smaller than I expected, almost goatlike. The glass eyes had an accusing stare.

I glanced over the bookshelf beneath the row of mounted heads. My eyes took in a few titles—*On Hunting the Gryffon; Common Remedies for Balancing the Physical Temperament; Mastery of Man: the Perils of Sorcery and the Summoning of Demons*—before turning my attention to the room's most curious décor.

In front of the window stood a writing desk, and on top of that, a dome of glass, covered in a film of dust. I brushed it off with my sleeve, revealing little wax garden fairies, posed on branches and preserved flowers, eerie in their realism.

I leaned in closer, disturbed but curious.

My stomach dropped, and every hair on my arms rose. Suddenly, I knew—these fairies weren't wax; they were taxidermy, too. Even though they were only garden fairies, with black bug eyes and smooth silvery bodies that reminded me of frogs', with no relation to the great fairies that so resembled humans, I trembled to see their tiny toes and fingers, pinned carefully to their forked brown twig forever. Thousands of tiny scales on their wings still shimmered softly in the light, but their little faces were dull; their poses too stiff for a living creature.

I turned away from the glass dome, feeling twisted inside.

The desk was free of paper or any evidence of recent use. *This must have been his father's study.*

What did most people keep close? Pictures and mementoes of people they loved, icons of their religion. I wondered what sort of man Mr. Parry's father had been, that he had wished to keep the fairies within sight of his desk. It was clear he had little respect for magical creatures. Perhaps he enjoyed seeing them imprisoned.

I threw open the top drawer, finding blank paper and a nubby pencil, keeping my eyes down, down, anything not to look at those fairies again. As I hurried from the room, Mr. Parry was just rounding the corner.

"Nimira," he said, taking in the papers in my hand. "Why, you should have told me you needed stationery. I thought you'd be outside enjoying the sunshine."

I was greatly relieved he assumed I was writing letters, as I'd forgotten every possible use for pencil and paper besides communicating with living automatons. "Oh—oh, yes. I do very much want to enjoy the sunshine, I just thought ... well, I promised Polly I'd let her know how I was."

"I wondered if—that is, it's such a lovely day ..." He clasped his hands behind his back. "If you'd like to take a picnic to the lawn."

"A picnic! Oh, but"—But what? I couldn't tell him about the automaton—"but that would be lovely."

"I thought you were the sort of girl for picnics. I've already asked my butler to bring it out to us. Let's go." He took the pencil and paper from my hands and set them aside on some useless hall furniture. I hoped I could play my part while the poor automaton wound down, still waiting for my return.

Mr. Parry and I walked outside to the gardens. A symmetrical path led around the flowers and trimmed bushes. The rains of recent days had left the plants lush with life. I brought my hand over my brow to shield my eyes from the sunshine. My nose filled with the fragrance of moist grass, living soil, and blooming flowers, from great pink roses to tiny white blossoms. Bees rushed by about their business while butterflies drifted on languid wings.

"Do you like the gardens?" he asked.

"I love all gardens," I said. "Even the humblest garden is welcome when you live in the city."

"What were your court gardens like, in Tassim?"

I struggled to remember details I could give him. The gardens of my childhood had dimmed to dreams of water playing over stones, twisting trees, serene expanses of grass. "They were full of mysteries and secrets, like . . . like poems turned into landscapes."

"'Poems turned into landscapes,'" he murmured with a slight smile. "And what of Vestenveld's gardens? Do you see poems in them?"

"Your gardens are like your country's poetry. Very frilly and organized."

We walked underneath a bower crawling with vines, to a spread of lawn scattered with shadows where the servants had already left a blanket and basket. The music of the wind shuddering through the copse of trees before moved me deep within. I had always found the sound rather mournful. The garden lay behind us, and from here the bees were a haze above the bright clusters of flowers. Beyond, the house stood sentry, with its many arches and chimneys and windows. The automaton rested behind one of those windows . . . could he see me? Did he think I'd betrayed him?

Mr. Parry sat on the blanket, carefully, like he didn't quite know how to sit on the ground. When he saw me sit, tucking my feet under me, he made a face.

"What is it?" I smiled.

"You just—look very foreign, in that pose. Very beguiling."

"Oh." I had been hoping he found me charming, or at least pleasant company, but "beguiling" was almost too much.

His lashes, so much darker than his hair, lowered. "I apologize, I've let my tongue run away from me." His eyes kept rising to me as he turned to the pitcher. "Lemonade?"

"Certainly, sir."

He poured. I unpacked plates and cutlery from the basket. A dragonfly zipped by, glistening jewel green. If life could always be like this, I should hardly complain. We filled our plates with sandwiches, cold potatoes dressed in vinegar, and sugared berries.

I wondered if the automaton had wound down yet. If he was alive, where had he come from? Had he always been alive? Was he a man trapped in an automaton's body, or a ghost who haunted it?

I noticed Mr. Parry also looked to the house. We both turned to each other. His expression was odd.

"So, you found my father's study," he said.

"I'm sorry. I should have told you I wanted paper."

He leaned back on an elbow and took a bite of sandwich. "Not at all. I only would have warned you. That room terrified me as a child. I had nightmares in which that unicorn would chase me."

"Why do you keep it, then?"

"Superstition, I suppose. My father took a lot of pride in his trophies. I'd rather have the unicorn than my father's ghost."

I couldn't tell whether he was teasing or not. "Your father really killed a unicorn?"

"So he said." Mr. Parry looked at the sky, blue and nearly cloudless now. "Did you have sorcerers in Tassim?"

"Of course. The healer Abraja and his apprentice, and a very old prophet, although few of his prophesies amounted to much. I used to hide from him—he had a stump instead of a left hand, and he spit when he talked."

"You don't have fairies in Tassim, do you?"

"No, sir. I don't think I've ever seen one."

"Yes, I thought so. They're all over here now." He sounded displeased.

"Where did they come from?"

"Oh, the same place my people came from, I suppose. The Old World. My mother said that when she was a little girl back in Salcy, fairies still lived in the great forests, and in the forests and hidden places all over the continent, but I think they've all been killed or come here by now."

"Are fairies much trouble?" I asked.

"They have been in the past. Magical creatures often are. I suppose you wouldn't know the history, but you came across the ocean, so you must know of the merfolk."

I nodded. If ships didn't pay for the privilege of sailing the seas, fish-tailed sirens would charm crew and passengers alike, leading them to their deaths. When I sailed to Lorinar, the captain tossed a bag of gold overboard to appease the merfolk, but even afterward some of the passengers had whispered nervously until we reached the safety of deeper waters. "Are the fairies like the mers, then? They demand things?"

"Not quite like the mers. The mers are born of the sea, and we're people of the land, so we're at a disadvantage in a ship. The fairies are born of the earth, so we share their land."

"And men have trouble sharing land," I said. I knew little of Lorinarian history, but every nation had its wars. Tiansher itself had been under another country's thumb for nearly a century and fought for independence in my great-grandfather's day.

"The trouble is, fairies have a different view of land than we do. You couldn't get any business done or progress made with fairies around. And they'll tromp all over a man's land—hunt on it, even— without any regard for property rights. *They* say we can't just own land, but can you imagine a world where men can't claim land to farm on? Could you imagine, having a picnic and suddenly a whole dozen fairies are roaming around, as if this were a public park? Thankfully, my father helped drive the heathens back past the river and erected the Western Wall before I was born."

Heathens—I bristled at that word. I'd had it hurled my way one too many times. "Some would say that people of my country are just heathens."

He spread out sideways on the blanket, propping his chin in his hand. "Oh, Nimira, I hardly think that of you. When I say heathens, I don't mean humans. *We* are all born of God, even if we call him different names, but fairies are born of the dirt beneath our feet."

"What does that mean? Do fairy babies grow like carrots?"

He laughed. "It just means they're different from us. They're tied to the land. It gives them power, and in return, they are bound to it."

His words unsettled me. "Fairies look just like humans in photographs. How can you tell them apart?"

"You often can't. A few fairies still live in our smaller cities and countrysides. But humans can live anywhere in the world, in cities of steel if they wish. Fairies wouldn't survive in our modern cities."

"I wonder that we aren't killing ourselves in those cities of steel," I said.

"You must admit, it's a testament to human tenacity that we can survive in any condition," Mr. Parry said. "Fairies aren't free like we are."

"But don't they have cities?"

"Oh, they do, very attractive cities, I'll admit, from the pictures. Lots of gardens and not a tenement to be found. But they're backward."

"Backward? It sounds like an improvement over New Sweeling, at least."

He scoffed. "No gas, no electricity, none of our modern progress."

"We didn't have those things in my country either. What's the good of modern progress if you haven't any gardens?"

"I'm sure your country will have these things in time. The fairies choose not to have them. Their barbarism is willful." He smiled with some impatience. "Oh, I don't suppose you'd understand these things."

I'd been in awe of Lorinar's "modern progress" when I'd first arrived, dazzled by street cars and the electric lights in many of New Sweeling's buildings, but I wondered if it had really helped anyone. In Tiansher, at least beggars and princes alike had the same priceless view of the Shai Mountains. "Well, sir, I still think I'd like to see a fairy city, to compare."

"Perhaps someday you shall," he said. "But first you should see Sormesen, and Heinlede, and Kassow . . ."

I smiled as I plucked grapes from their stems. "I doubt I'll ever travel so far as that!"

He looked up at the endless spread of sky, perhaps thinking, as I was, how we shared that sky with all those far-flung places. "When Annalie passed, one of my greatest regrets was that I could never explore the world with her. We meant to travel. Instead, I've never even left the boundaries of Lorinar." He met my eyes. "Someday, Nimira."

The intimate way he spoke my name so stirred my nerves that I couldn't speak.

"For now, I must content myself with words and pictures. Tell me more of your country."

6

We talked long enough for Mr. Parry's pale nose to turn pink in the sun.

"I told you picnics were nothing but a hazard," Miss Rashten scolded as he entered. "Not only have you ruined your complexion, but there are all manner of insects; why, I've even heard of a picnic set upon by bandits."

"Thankfully we seem to have escaped that fate," Mr. Parry said.

Grumbling, she hustled off and came back shortly with some concoction of lemon juice and rosewater, prattling on about its usefulness while she tried to administer it to Mr. Parry's nose.

I wondered if I could yet slip away to the automaton.

"Let's go to the library and see about animals," Mr. Parry said. We had been talking of elephants and tigers. "I think I may have a book with pictures."

The automaton would have wound down anyway, I told myself, and I must not begrudge Mr. Parry's attentions. I was living the

dream of all trouser girls who made wishes on stars from their gar-
rets or spun fancies while they mended their dancing slippers.

We gave the whole afternoon over to looking at books and
talking of the mourning habits of elephants, the holidays of our
respective nations, our dear departed mothers, and the education
of women. We were always polite.

I didn't know what to think about Mr. Parry. Sometimes I was
taken with him, his flashing smiles, his dark eyes, his esteem for
me and my intelligence. When he spoke to me I never doubted
that he thought I had worth as a person; he didn't just see a trouser girl.

Other times, however . . . I knew nothing of fairies, but I didn't
like how he spoke of them. I thought of the garden fairies on
his father's desk, and wondered how much the son took after the
father.

The next morning, I tucked paper and pencil in the pocket of
my dress and returned to the automaton. I stood behind him, staring at the silver key for a long time. Knowing he had tried to communicate with me, winding him now seemed a very different matter.
I wondered if he could feel it.

Finally, I took a deep breath and slipped the key in its slot. I
saw life fill his eyes as I came around to stand before him.

I spoke right away. "I'm so sorry. I met Mr. Parry in the hall
yesterday while fetching the paper and he asked me to a picnic. I
couldn't very well refuse. If he knew I'd seen you come alive, he'd
send me away like all the rest."

"Mmm."

"We don't have long." I tore off a scrap of paper and wedged it
between two keys. "I'm marking the midpoint of the alphabet here
so I can count letters faster. I've made a chart of the letters—the

first half above this line, the second half below it. Don't actually play the keys or you'll make a good deal of noise—just touch them." I hoped I wasn't explaining things too fast. I was quite frantic that Mr. Parry might burst in, or one of the maids—especially Miss Rashten. "Can you do that?"

"Mmm-mmm!"

"All right." I propped the chart of letters up where the piano book would go and stood at his shoulder with my pencil and paper. His left hand jerked to life, sliding to a key. His mechanism clicked and knocked inside his breast. He gently tapped a key, and I checked it against the chart.

"*G*," I said, writing it down, and as soon as I spoke it, the hand turned to the next letter. Tedious progress, yet I doubt I'd have noticed the moments pass if not for my fear of discovery. Curiosity made my limbs tremble.

G-A-R-V-I-N, I wrote. "Garvin? You mean the old ambassador of magic?"

"Mm." He resumed spelling. DEAD? He made a questioning noise.

"Um . . . well, yes. They're saying he was killed by fairy bandits." He grunted with distress. TELL MORE.

"There's a new ambassador now. Mr. Smollings, I believe. I don't really know any more. Why? Did you know Garvin?"

He made a thinking noise, then an affirmative one. *He knew Garvin, but I think not well*, I noted on my paper. I glanced at the clock. Already, five minutes gone by for these few questions. I had so many more, but how much time could I take? If Mr. Parry came in, I'd have a hard time explaining myself. Before I could decide what to ask next, the hands began to move again. I quickly searched the chart of letters.

FREE ME.

I don't know why I felt like someone had grabbed my heart and shook it. I looked at him, into the glass eyes framed with dainty false lashes. The eyes looked back. The trapped thing inside them pleaded. I could almost read his thoughts. *You're the only chance I have.* "What can I do?" I asked.

FIND KARSTOR, he spelled.

"Karstor? Who . . . what . . . is that?"

SORCER—

I heard the wood floor groan in the hall and stopped writing. I shoved the paper under the stack of song sheets until the footsteps passed.

"Sorcerer?" I whispered.

"Mmm."

"I can't talk to you much longer. One more question for today, and then we must sing and play before anyone grows suspicious at how quiet we are. What are you? A man? A ghost?"

Here came the longest response yet. A MAN, FAIR LADY. A MAN.

7

A man, fair lady. A man.

In my mind, the words had a voice.

He was a man. Not a ghost—at least, not as I imagined ghosts to be. He didn't want to scare me. He wanted my help.

How frustrated he must have been, trying to communicate with all those other ladies, only to see them scream and tear from the room, as I had nearly done. But I hadn't, and now I must be the one to learn his story.

I sang the frivolous tunes of Lorinar. He plucked out his haunting notes with the strange timing of an automaton, as if he really were only a machine. Before I left him, he touched the keys again to say GOOD-BYE. Then his chest moved back, his hands stilled, the eyes dulled. He slept.

I turned to the door. I didn't want to look upon him anymore, with the life gone from him.

Linza brought lunch to my room, offering her small smile and a plate of cold roast and potatoes. Her sleeves were rolled up above her elbows, wiry arms ending in chapped hands. I imagined her scrubbing the dainty breakfast plates and great pots.

"Would you like something for your hands?" I said. "I have a little cream left from last winter. My hands dry out in the cold." I wished I could tell her about the automaton, but I didn't dare tell a soul.

"Oh, you're too good to me, miss!" she said, but with such eagerness that I knew she'd accept. I opened the valise with my scant possessions from the troupe. I had not touched it since I'd arrived. My mother's sky blue bird costume lay across the top, and Linza gasped at the sight of it.

"Did you dance in that?" she asked, peering over my shoulder at the deep blue sash.

"Oh, no. These clothes belonged to my mother. In the troupe, we wore a modified costume—not quite like what we'd wear at home."

"It's lovely," Linza breathed.

I was about to close the lid when I noticed the eagerness in Linza's eyes.

Many girls would have only scorned the tunic and trousers, but I held them up for Linza's inspection. She ran her rough fingers over the embroidery.

"Lovely needlework," she said.

I smiled. "Some other women in court were much better still. My mother was impatient with the needle."

"No, I adore it. May I spread this out on the bed?"

At my nod, Linza unfurled the sash across my quilt. She studied the curling designs, her lips just parted.

I always kept Mother's slippers in their dyed leather shoe bag, but now I drew them out and placed them in Linza's hands. "She did her best work here," I said. "Wedding shoes. She wore them only once."

"Oh, miss, was your mother a *princess*?" She turned the slippers over, admiring every embroidered inch from vamp to soles. Jewel-toned trees and birds, hills and waves danced across them, including a deer with a missing leg. It was customary to include one purposeful mistake in every design, and as a child, the mistakes had delighted me most.

"No princess," I said. "A dancer in the royal troupe. We had only one princess."

"Did you ever see her?"

"Of course. You would be disappointed, though. She was ugly."

Linza laughed. "I guess real princesses are never like in the stories. Have you seen the princess of Roscardi?"

"No."

"She was here last year, and her picture was in the paper, and oh—she looked frightened and sickly. Like this." Linza sucked in her cheeks and widened her eyes, an alarming expression, as Linza's eyes already verged on buglike.

"Princesses are people like the rest of us, I suppose."

She handed the slippers back with a sigh. "Oh, Miss Nimira, you have such pretty things. I wish I could embroider like that. I'm terrible with sewing and mending. Rashten—that is, *Miss* Rashten scolds me about it."

"Well, embroidery is more satisfying than mending. You're creating something beautiful."

"That's true." Linza made a face, probably thinking of her work, which I imagined was rarely beautiful. "But I can't complain. Mr. Parry takes care of us. My mother worked for him before I did, and even now, with her rheumatism as bad as it is, he set her up right."

"I'm glad of that, anyway." I handed her the little jar of cream. "For your hands."

She took a dab and worked it in. "You should eat, miss, before it's cold."

"It was cold to begin with!"

She shook her head at herself. I put the clothes away and Linza returned to her tasks, but if the food was cold, the room had warmed with company.

⸻

As soon as I wound the automaton the next morning, he began to spell.

"Wait, wait!" I cried. "Let me arrange things."

I wondered what he might tell me today. Maybe he knew more about Garvin's disappearance, or—

WHAT IS YOUR N—

I cut him off. "My name?"

"Mmm."

I stared at the sentence I had just taken so much time to write. He must have had a thousand things to say, yet he wanted to know my name first? "You could have just spelled 'name.' I'd have known what you meant. But it's Nimira. You could call me Nim, though. It's shorter."

I LIKE NIM.

My stomach flipped. I could hardly bear kind words from him; it would have been easier if he showed no emotion, no opinion. "You hardly know Nim."

THE NAME. I started to respond, but he was still going.

SILLY GIRL. He finished with an emphatic grunt, a verbal exclamation mark.

"I'm not silly," I said, but my words sounded so strange, spoken to his still face. I quickly looked back at his hands. "We have important work to do, and not much time. We must figure out what I can do to set you free."

I'M ERRIS. PLEASURE TO MEET YOU.

I almost scolded him for taking the time to write all that out, but then I realized he must have been yearning for this simple, normal thing: an exchange of names and greetings. I wondered how long he had waited to tell someone his name.

"Erris," I said. "I like Erris, too."

Only now did he return to business. KARSTOR, he repeated.

"You said he was a sorcerer, but where can I find him? Who is he?"

COUNCIL.

"The Sorcerer's Council? I know Mr. Parry mentioned it. The ambassador of magic is head of the council, right?"

SPEAK ONLY TO KARSTOR. His hands jerked around so fast I could hardly keep up.

"Why? What's going on? Who are you?" Strange enough that the automaton had consciousness, but he seemed to have rather urgent business with these sorcerers as well.

He made an unsure sound. GARVIN SAID TELL ONLY KARSTOR.

"Did you know Garvin when you were a man?"

AUTOMATON.

"You were already an automaton?"

YES.

"Did you talk to Garvin with the piano, too?"

SOME, BEFORE.

"He died?"

"Mmm." He sounded sad.

"You've never come alive for Mr. Parry," I said.

CAN'T TRUST. ONLY KARSTOR.

"But I'm not Karstor. How do you know you can trust me?"

I DON'T, he said. BUT MUST TRUST SOMEONE.

I jumped at the sound of a door shutting somewhere in the distance and quickly motioned for him to start playing. He obliged, starting a merry tune, ending our conversation for that day.

I kept the papers with the words I'd written hidden in my valise. I took them out and stared at them more times than I cared to admit. In this way, I managed to keep up the conversation over several days without forgetting what to say next.

I asked where he'd come from.

TELMIRRA, he spelled.

"I feel I've heard of it ... in a story ..."

WEST. OUR CAPITAL.

"The fairy capital? Are you a fairy?"

YES.

I thought I hid my surprise well, finding he was one of the fairies Mr. Parry had warned me of. Or, at least, he had been. "What happened to you?"

ENCHANTMENT.

"How long ago?"

He hesitated. TOO LONG.

"Years?"

He disregarded my question. GARVIN'S DEATH SUSPICIOUS.

"Why? What do you mean? Oh, you probably don't have time to answer anyway." I could have cried with frustration for how slowly the answers trickled from his fingers.

NOT FAIRIES.

"There are fairy bandits, though, aren't there? I don't mean to insult your—your people. I'm not sure I'd blame them, sometimes. But if I'm going to help you, I need to know at least a little of what's going on."

He hesitated. I COULD BE WRONG. TIMES CHANGED.

"Did fairies and humans get along better in the past?"

THERE WAS PEACE ONCE. NO WALL. His faint exhalation sounded sad.

"I suppose war always comes at some point when countries are neighbors. Especially if fairies and humans are so different."

"Mmm," he agreed. I THINK GARVIN WAS KILLED TO PREVENT ALLIANCE.

"Alliance with the fairies?"

YES.

"Who would do such a thing? Who are his rivals?"

COUNCIL.

"The Sorcerer's Council?"

"Mmm."

"But Garvin was the head of the council. Are you saying it was a conspiracy?"

NOT SURE.

"And Garvin died before he got a chance to free you?"

"Mmm . . ." Regret infused his only sound.

8

That evening, I dined again with Mr. Parry in the tower room. I knew I must not think of Erris, must not ponder what I'd ask him when we next spoke, or what his answers would be. Mr. Parry must think he held all my attention, or everything would unravel.

"Did you practice with the automaton this morning, Miss Nimira?"

"Hmm? Oh. Yes. Yes, of course."

"He hasn't started howling and waving his arms around?" Mr. Parry smirked.

"Oh, no, sir. He's been very well behaved." I gathered peas onto my spoon.

"How stiff you sound. I thought we'd moved past that at the picnic. I'd like you to feel comfortable around me."

"Oh, Mr. Parry, I assure you I am quite comfortable."

"You can call me Hollin. Maybe that will help."

I doubted it.

"I've sent for the dressmaker from Pelswater to make you a gown," he said. "For your performances."

"A gown! How exciting; I've never owned a gown." I tried to summon the appropriate enthusiasm. I might have been excited at any other time.

"Unfortunately, I'm not sure we'll have it before Mr. Smollings pays a visit. He'll be coming sooner than I expected. He's eager to see the automaton." For all Hollin's talk of my stiffness, he said this in a very scripted tone.

"Oh?" I had a dreadful suspicion this could be more than idle curiosity. "And he is an old friend of yours?"

"Not *my* old friend," he corrected. "He was a friend of my father's. Since he is head of the Sorcerer's Council, an office to which I aspire . . . we must make him welcome, however unpleasant his company might be."

Unpleasant? Oh dear. Mention of the Sorcerer's Council already struck dread within my heart.

"What does the Sorcerer's Council do?" I asked, hoping to gather insight.

"They set the rules for magical usage in Lorinar, and handle diplomacy with the magical races. The fairies, particularly, since we have the most trouble with them."

"What sort of trouble is it, exactly? I thought you said they were driven back behind the wall during the war, before you were born."

"Well, yes, but they still control the western trade routes and the taxes they've imposed on us—" He stopped abruptly. "It's all very dull and political, Nimira, I don't suppose you really care to hear it. Besides, with a firm hand like Smollings in charge, we can be sure the fairies will think twice before they act upon us."

"I don't understand. Didn't you just say you found Smollings's company unpleasant?"

Hollin lifted his brows. "Well, so I do. Good politicians can be very unpleasant people. But something must be done. Garvin was in favor of a generous alliance with the fairies. One can only shudder at the thought."

I thought this made Garvin's disappearance sound all the more suspicious, but I didn't see how I could inquire further, or Hollin might wonder at my interest. With Mr. Smollings on the way, I didn't want to draw any attention to myself, lest Erris be discovered.

Hollin poured himself something to drink. "Goodness, Nimira, you are certainly interested in heavy matters."

I tried to look innocent, which is probably never a good idea. "I hate to sound ignorant on matters that may be important to you."

"When I'm with you, I want to forget all that." A gentle smile quirked his lips. "If you are innocent of all this, you should remain so. Keep to your books and your gardens."

I thought of how Mother behaved in court—both feminine and unflappable, with compliments for everyone who counted. She was a different person when she came to tell me stories before I went to sleep, and another person with her dearest friends, when she complained about the same people she praised. I knew Mother would have found some other way to learn about the fairies and the Sorcerer's Council.

I felt a little sick, but pretending was a woman's lot, more than ever on foreign soil. "Very well, sir, although some might say books are hardly innocent." I tried to sound teasing.

"You sound like my Anni," he said. I didn't like the way he said it, "my Anni," so intimate, like they had just spoken.

"How long has she been . . . gone, sir?" I asked.

"Almost two years."

"I'm sorry. Miss Rashten told me she was quite young."

"Eighteen, yes. She would have turned twenty in March."

"And she . . . took an illness?"

"Fever. Very sudden."

I heard guilt in his voice. "That isn't your fault, you know."

I saw him tuck his pain back inside. "I want to begin again, you see," he said. "I wanted such a simple thing. To see the world with my wife at my side. I would trade Vestenveld for a cottage if I could have that." He straightened a little. "I'm sorry. Let's talk of other things."

"I understand, sir." I think I was just as relieved to change the subject.

And so we talked of the opera, and he promised to take me someday.

9

"Erris, what happened to trap you here? How did you become an automaton?" I was full of curiosity.

WE WERE AT WAR.

"Does that mean you've been an automaton for thirty years? Hollin said the last conflict was thirty years ago."

He sighed. POSSIBLY.

I could hardly grasp the idea of being imprisoned between life and death for thirty years. Everyone he knew would have aged. Many would have died.

"So you were at war, and someone did this to you?"

ENEMIES.

"I gathered it wasn't your friends.... Was that the Sorcerer's Council's doing as well?"

YES. I WAS CAPTURED.

"Why did they turn you into an automaton? Why didn't they just kill you?"

MAYBE THEY WANTED ME ALIVE BUT HELPLESS. NOT SURE. ONE MINUTE I WAS ME, AND THEN—

"You woke in this form?"

"Mmm."

"How awful." I couldn't imagine the horror of waking up in a different body, one that wasn't even really a body at all ... with movement and speech suddenly snatched from my grasp.

"You're very brave," I murmured.

NO, he replied. I'M SCARED. TRAPPED. CAN'T SHOW IT. NO POINT ANYWAY.

When I started to respond, he made an anxious catch in his throat. Like he couldn't stand my pity. I understood that, but the only proper response seemed to be pity or nothing. So I said nothing.

I WANT TO SPEAK TO YOU. WITH A VOICE.

"I know."

I felt like I could have peeled back the stiff fingers and found living ones beneath. If I could only see the spark of life in him and draw it out. If I could only strike his back and make him breathe. I ached to see his eyes searching from within his frozen face.

I sat on the edge of the piano bench beside him. There was hardly room. I angled out one foot to keep my perch. His arm bumped mine. I jumped.

"Mm," he said softly, like he was sorry for having scared me.

I put my finger to his cheek. It was cold and hard. I trailed a line down to his chin. "When I touch you, do you feel it?"

"Mmm."

Erris couldn't even see much of me, when I sat beside him. His head couldn't turn. He couldn't move to touch me in return. I let my finger drift to his ear, so finely formed. I traced the outer curve, momentarily transfixed by the idea that my touch could travel through this magic and reach him, just like a living man.

He started to spell. STOP.

I sprung up from the bench, heart racing, like I had committed a crime. "I'm sorry."

He spelled something else, but I didn't catch it at first. I had to ask him to begin again, although I hated to.

He grunted with some frustration. SIT AGAIN. When I didn't move, he added, PLEASE.

I lowered myself back onto the bench. "I'm sorry," I said again. "I didn't mean to to—I'm not sure what came over me."

N-O. I easily recognized those letters in a glance. ONLY . . . YOU MAKE ME MISS . . .

The sentence remained unfinished. I twirled the pencil around and around, like the warriors of Tiansher twirled their scimitars in parades. Of course, I knew all the things he must miss. Movement. Freedom. Food. Speech. Life.

Erris played one note to snatch back my attention. DON'T BE SAD.

My thoughts blurred. I didn't want to feel this way. I had to gather my emotions. I had to stop. This wasn't right.

NEVER WANT TO UPSET YOU. YOU BRING ME HAPPINESS.

I stared at the letters I'd written. He must have been aching inside, a hundred times worse than I ached for him, but he worried that he'd upset me. He didn't ask for sympathy.

"I *am* going to bring you more than happiness," I said. "I'm going to help you. You'll speak to me with a voice yet."

I wished I believed my own words.

10

The dressmaker came: a wispy, exhausted woman who spoke every word like a scolding. She stuck me with pins. I wondered if she treated her Lorinarian customers this way. Hollin ordered me things I hardly thought necessary, unless he meant for me to stay through winter at the least: a new coat, a walking outfit with a shorter skirt and black braiding at the sleeves, and, of course, the ball gown.

It was to be made of pink silk, trimmed around the plunging neckline with velvet flowers in black and cream.

"Miss Rashten thinks pink doesn't suit my complexion," I warned him.

"Nonsense," he said. "There is no color more feminine than pink; no woman it does not suit, and you especially, with your golden glow."

I gave him a demure smile; what else could one do?

In truth, I didn't have to feign excitement over the new clothes, especially the gown, seeing those yards of silk. I had never owned anything so grown-up and lovely, nor so expensive. When I dreamed of walking onstage in that gown, my imaginary audience forgot I was foreign, so dazzled were they by my majesty. I sang the best performance of my life. Why, every trouser girl in Lorinar found themselves work in the better halls, following the wake of my success!

As I said, at night I dream of things I scoff at by day.

The dressmaker worked her sewing machine from sunrise to sunset, while the servants stepped up their own efforts, preparing Vestenveld for Mr. Smollings's arrival. The bedrooms were aired, the floors swept, and the furniture dusted. The maids even braved Hollin's father's study. I took to dressing my own hair in a simple coiled braid just to spare poor Linza this one task, and I gave her my jar of hand cream. "I believe you'll need it more than I do."

He came in the night, after I had gone to bed. I heard faint voices from the main hall, and imagined Miss Rashten there with her lamp and clucking tongue, and Hollin giving dour greetings. I pulled the covers up to my nose. I had heard enough about Smollings that I wasn't exactly looking forward to meeting him.

When I woke, the men had already left to hunt. Linza brought my breakfast tray without a word or a smile.

"Linza, what's wrong?"

"I'm worn out to the bone, miss, if you'll pardon me saying so. And all this for—!" She huffed. "I'm sorry. I'm letting my mouth run on."

"For Mr. Smollings? What's the trouble with him?"

She glanced both ways, as if someone might pop up from behind the furniture, and dropped her voice to a whisper. "He scares me worse than that clockwork man."

I drew closer to her, lowering my own voice. "Mr. Parry said something similar. That he was unpleasant. Even before I came here, I heard rumors," I lied, hoping to encourage her into telling me more.

She nodded eagerly. "I'm sure I've heard the same!"

"Have you?" I wondered if anyone else thought Garvin's disappearance might not have been fairies after all.

"They say he washes his face with ghost powder!"

I suppressed a snort. Hardly the revelation I hoped for. "What on earth is ghost powder?"

"They sell it at the apothecary," Linza said. "I think it's to strengthen one's power in the dark arts."

"How do you get powder from a ghost?"

"I don't know..." Linza looked a little crestfallen that I had disparaged her story.

"Well, whatever it is, it sounds very sinister." I brushed off my skepticism. I hated to hurt Linza's feelings.

Linza smoothed back loose wisps of her hair and peered at me curiously. "What rumors did you hear?"

"Oh..." I waved my hand. "Just similar things about dark magic. I should let you go. You need your rest."

I lingered over my eggs and toast, heaving a few dramatic sighs to myself. If one spends too many hours in solitude, one starts to emote for one's own benefit.

When I left my room, the halls were as still and silent as catacombs. For days, more maids than I'd known existed at Vestenveld had rushed about, carrying linens or brandishing dusters, but now I might have been the only person in the house. I supposed they had all withdrawn to the servants' quarters, or maybe the cook needed help in the kitchens. I went and wound Erris.

He spelled my name in greeting. NIM.

I looked out the window to the garden. I didn't see the men, not that I expected to, but the gardener was pruning, and seeing another soul brought me comfort. Behind me, Erris began to play, a tune both lively and urgent. He stopped when I turned. I frowned at him. "You shouldn't play songs that aren't part of our repertoire! Someone might *hear*."

"Mmm?" His tone expressed concern.

"I'm sorry if I snapped. It's just—the house feels different since the visitors came."

YES.

"Do you sense it, too? I haven't even met them yet. They're off hunting birds, I think."

FOR SPORT.

Of course fairies wouldn't hunt for sport. I hated to think of Hollin shooting down beautiful birds. "I don't know that Hollin enjoys it much," I said, trying to convince myself. "He even told me Mr. Smollings is a good politician, but unpleasant company."

TRULY.

I was growing accustomed to counting out letters; I hardly needed to write them anymore, although I kept at it for my records. "I hardly blame him. You should see this house, Erris. His father turned real tigers to gold, and now they guard the gate, and he even has the head of a unicorn in his study and . . . worse."

"Mmm?" His voice was low.

For a moment, I wished I had said nothing. I thought it might be better not to know. But then, it must be worse to be trapped in one room, without any idea where you were beyond those four walls. Like a devoted nurse at the bed of a paralyzed man, I brought a wisp of life to the stiff arms and the fairy shoes frozen fast to the ground. I described the hall ceiling that stretched so high that ghosts could have waltzed in the rafters, dear Linza and the sniping comments of Miss Rashten, even the horror of discovering the garden fairies frozen under glass in his father's study.

Erris's hands quivered at this, but he didn't reply.

"I'm sorry," I said. "I didn't know if I should tell you."

YES. DO.

"I thought you'd want to know."

I MISS MY FATHER. HE'D KNOW WHAT TO DO.

"Is he still alive?"

NO . . .

"I'm sorry. I understand. You must miss home terribly."

I DO. He made a sound in his throat rather like a sigh. I SHOULD BE MORE SAD. FEELS LIKE A DREAM.

"I guess you never had a proper good-bye." I recalled my own good-bye with Father. I'd been furious with him for long months, with good reason, yet when I said good-bye, I sobbed like anything. He said he was sorry and kissed my cheek. I said I would write. At the time, I'd meant it heartily, and consoled myself with my dream of a triumphant return with pockets full of gold, but I'd been a naïve young thing. "But, then again . . . perhaps saying good-bye doesn't change anything."

His arms spread across the piano keys, and drew together again, wavering a moment before he began to spell. YOU LOOK SAD.

I quickly shook my head.

An unexpected chuckle carried down the hall. "Play!" I hissed, as I snatched the marking paper from the piano. Male conversation drew close. Erris began a melody.

The door flung open. Hollin entered, followed by a man clad in a dark gray suit with pointed sorcerer's cuffs on his jacket.

"Ah," he said. "So this is the automaton..."

Hollin stepped beside me to make introductions. "And this is Nimira, the singer I've hired. Nimira, this is Mr. Soleran Smollings."

Smollings was handsome for an older man, dark and thin, with distinguished high cheekbones and a straight narrow nose. His eyes swept over me, appraising and unreadable.

"Charming, but next time I should like to see her in trousers," he said. "Quite odd to see a little girl from Tassim in one of our ladies' fine dresses."

I forced myself to keep quiet. Nothing good could come of arguing, but his condescending words were almost more than I could bear.

"Don't insult her," Hollin said, dark eyes flashing anger.

"Oh, Parry," Smollings said. "If I didn't know better, I'd think you a little moon-eyed." He smiled at me, as if a mere smile would soothe my shallow foreign feelings. I hated for Erris to hear them deride me. Cheerful tunes came from the piano as we spoke; of course Erris must play until his mechanism wound down.

Now Smollings went to stand behind Erris while he finished his song. As he watched Erris, I watched him. He ran his hand along Erris's arm. He peered into his glass eyes, giving his cheek a brief, appraising stab with one finger. He lifted aside his coat to see his clockwork slowly turning. I wanted to shove him away.

Hollin rubbed his hands, as if they were cold. "Lovely craftsmanship, isn't it?"

"It has been too many months since I've paid a visit to Vestenveld." Smollings's hand lingered on Erris's back, near his keyhole. "I've been so busy. Where did you find this automaton, Parry?"

"An auction. I was looking for new furniture when this caught my eye."

"You know, I heard the Pelerine family recently sold Garvin's Colsom Lake estate and all its contents. You attended that auction, didn't you? Fidinch said he saw you there."

"Well, yes, it was at that sale, now that you mention it."

"I didn't know he had an *automaton*," Smollings said, as if it meant something particular to own an automaton. "I wonder how he came by it. But then, what do I know of his personal possessions?"

Erris had stopped playing, and he made his usual move before winding down—sitting back and surveying his nonexistent audience. Smollings let the coat drop from his hand and withdrew a step. Hollin looked at him curiously, and Smollings answered with a slight shrug. "Shall we wind him again? Let's see your little songbird perform."

Hollin nodded and took Erris's key from his pocket.

Smollings reached. "May I wind him?"

Hollin hesitated only for a moment. "I don't see why not."

I stood in wait, clenching my fists behind my skirt, as Smollings took the key, running his thumb along its length. He pushed aside the coat, peering deep into the heart of Erris's body, pausing like he expected something to happen before he jabbed the key in. He wound slowly. We both watched him.

"That should do," Hollin said, lifting his hand. "Have a seat."

As Erris came to life once more, Smollings settled into a chair, lacing his fingers. Hollin remained standing, leaning a shoulder against the wall, his arms crossed.

Hollin's eyes were on me as I waited for my cue, but Smollings watched Erris. I looked up to the ceiling. I had never noticed before how ornate it was, with molded designs in a circular pattern around the light fixture. Erris began to play. I knew I must sing, showing no concern. Smollings already suspected Erris was no ordinary automaton—that was obvious.

"One windy day in autumn, I lost my darling dear . . ." My voice started out tremulous. *I must sing with passion, with feeling,* I reminded myself—like any great lady of the theaters and music halls. "He's gone away and left me, and now I linger here . . ."

When I finished, my arms dropped and my head ached, strangely spent.

Smollings gave me a few polite claps. "Hollin," he said. "Have you had this automaton looked over? To be sure it's free of curses, or enchantments?"

"I've looked him over," Hollin said, turning to Erris like he might see something new. He had wound down, but still I willed him not to move or make a sound.

"You sensed nothing out of the ordinary?"

"Of course not, or I would have said something, wouldn't I?" Hollin's voice remained measured, but I could tell he had grown a little impatient with Smollings's scrutiny. "Although, before I hired Nimira, I tried a couple of other girls, and both of them swore they saw it move and grunt, but I think they had overactive imaginations. I've wound it a hundred times and it does precisely the same thing every time. You've never seen anything unusual, have you, Nimira?"

I didn't dare meet Smollings's eyes. I tried to look shy. "No, sir."

"If it's haunted, wouldn't it have revealed itself to Nimira or myself by now?"

"Perhaps not, if it has something to hide." Smollings rubbed his fingers across his lips. "Did you ever hear the story that went around after the last Fairy War?"

"I vaguely recall it."

"It was before your time. I was just a young man myself. But after the execution of the fairy royals, one of the bodies was never found. The second-youngest prince. We'd occasionally get an alarming report in the papers that he had turned up and the fairies were sure to rally around him, only to hear the next week that it had been a mistake. The fairy lands were in chaos, battling for secession, but the lost prince never appeared, and of course the king's cousin finally took the throne."

"Yes?" Hollin said, glancing at Erris, obviously wondering what the connection could be to his automaton. I was getting an inkling, and reminded myself to keep breathing as a normal girl would.

"At one point it was rumored that the prince had been imprisoned inside the body of a clockwork man, by enemies within his own ranks."

Oh, God. I knew my face must be turning pale, and I quickly giggled before Mr. Smollings could notice my shock and question me.

"I see your songbird finds the tale amusing, Hollin," Smollings said, raising his voice in irritation.

"Well, come now!" I said. "Are you suggesting that this automaton is a lost fairy prince?"

It was easier to keep up my act when Hollin took my side. "It does sound far-fetched, Mr. Smollings, you must admit. This automaton cost me only five gold! Quite a bargain for a fairy prince."

"In the aftermath of the war, sorcerers combed the country, investigating every piece of clockwork they could find," Smollings said. "But how would we find him if he didn't want to be found? Or if someone was hiding him ... You may laugh now, but why would

Garvin Pelerine have this automaton? Tucked away in his summer house near the fairy borders, at that? Garvin Pelerine always was sympathetic to those heathen fairies. . . ."

"Did Garvin mean to reinstate the old fairy line?" Hollin asked. He looked unnerved by the prospect.

"I believe so," Smollings said. "Garvin always did talk like he'd bring about some grand new era of peace. As if it's even possible! I don't think the current fairy king would be too happy to see a true heir."

Hollin looked at Erris again, more carefully this time. His brows furrowed.

"But Garvin's gone," Hollin said finally. "How could we even find out if this is the theoretical fairy prince?"

"I daresay Garvin's only half gone as long as Karstor's still roaming around," Smollings said, and I almost jumped at the name. "They were always close as brothers. He's just returned from Heinlede, but I have no doubt they exchanged letters. Anything Garvin knew, Karstor probably knows. He'll be at Aldren Hall. We could show the automaton there, just as an entertainment. You can bring your little trouser girl along and all that, as if you don't suspect a thing, and just see how he reacts."

"What do we do with it, if it is the fairy prince?" Hollin asked.

"Naturally, we make what use of it we can," Smollings said. "Then we see that it's destroyed."

My heart skipped a beat at that terrible word, "destroyed," and then it beat fiercer than I had ever known, as something stirred within me. I would tear Smollings's eyes from his face before I let him destroy Erris. I would do anything I could.

Could it really come to that?

Hollin looked at Erris, and I made sure to stay composed as he moved on to me. Sympathy and frustration mingled in his eyes. He didn't like Smollings either, but he respected him, and therefore was not immune to his influence.

I must ensure that my influence was more important.

11

That night, I heard a girl scream.

I shot up in bed, throwing back the covers. Bare feet slapped down the hall, closer and closer. I rushed to the door. Linza? Sleep blurred my eyes. I flung open the door, and a caped figure barreled toward me, trailed by dim orbs of light that floated after her like fireflies. Her desperate cry filled my ears.

Not Linza.

I whirled back into my room, and she followed me in. She was upon me, wriggling her shoulders forward like a caterpillar, knocking me down onto my bed with the brute force of her head. At first I thought she had no arms at all.

No, no, they were only bound behind her.

"Help me," she said, barely more than a whisper. Her weight was on me. I could hardly see her face in the darkness, only that she could have been lovely—that her eyes gleamed wild in the moonlight. Her dark hair fell thick over her face and even tickled my own nose. The orbs danced around her face.

I tried to push her off me. She was stronger than I would have guessed.

"Stop—stop!" I said. I was trying to keep calm. I didn't know if I should scream for help.

I heard the men running down the hall. "She went down here!"

She spoke louder now, her voice low and slightly husky for a woman. "Please help," she begged, rolling off of me. "Please! Untie my hands. Hurry, hurry! He's coming."

"Who *are* you?"

Smollings burst in then, holding a sorcerer's staff aloft in his left hand like a torch. With his right, he yanked the girl to her feet and dragged her to the door. He placed the head of the staff against her shoulder. His clinical manner in the face of the girl's distress chilled me.

I got to my feet. "Who is she? Where are you taking her?"

The girl looked at me. "He's dangerous." She said it like a warning to me.

Smollings pressed the staff against her flesh. "One word and you'll feel it," he said. He shot a look at me. "Get back to bed. This doesn't concern you."

"No—who is she?" I could hardly ignore the woman's distress.

"Nobody. Don't listen to her, she's crazy. She doesn't know what she's going on about."

Smollings gave the girl's shoulder a mere tap with the staff. Light briefly flared from the top and she flinched with pain. Hollin ran into my room. He was still dressed in suit and necktie like he had never gone to bed. He breathed hard, and his eyes pleaded with me not to ask the questions that leaped to my lips.

"Let go of her, Smollings," he said. "She'll cooperate now." He didn't meet the girl's eyes. Or mine. "Please."

"She'd better," Smollings said. He lowered the staff, but his fingers still gripped her arm tightly as he ushered her from the room like a jealous lover.

"Nimira," Hollin said. "I'm—I'm sorry about that."

I pushed loose hairs back behind my ears. I wished I were not in my braids and white nightgown like a child. "Who was that?"

"She— You weren't supposed to see her."

"But as it stands, I could hardly miss seeing her. She asked for my help."

He looked at me without blinking. The corners of his lips had turned-down shadows. His eyes were dark caves between his high white forehead and his smooth, boyish cheeks.

"If you won't tell me who she is, what am I to think then?" I asked.

Hollin leaned out the doorway to see that Smollings had gone, and then he crossed the room to me. "You're the one person I wish to tell," he whispered. "If I could tell anyone."

"Then tell me!" I could hardly withhold my impatience.

"I'm in his debt," he said. "Smollings's influence and aid have kept me from losing everything I have. Only, they come at a price; there are things I cannot say."

He stood so close. He looked so sad. "I would keep your secrets. It can't be healthy, Hollin, to have so *many* secrets."

I thought he might kiss me, the way he looked at me. I didn't know how I would react. I read his desires in his eyes—he might wish for a tender hand at his cheek, or a sympathetic word.

"Smollings brought the girl," he said abruptly. "She is a . . . a witch. A madwoman. He's transporting her to the prison in New Sweeling."

"A witch? Where did she come from?"

He shook his head. "It doesn't matter. He arrested her on his travels. You mustn't tell anyone."

"Where did he get her? Why does he have her?"

Hollin's every word seemed to come at great effort. "I don't like it either. But I say nothing."

"But she was begging me to help her! He was *hurting* her, Hollin!"

"She's a criminal," Hollin said, his pale cheeks flushed.

I didn't know if I even believed him, or at least, what Smollings had told him. "Whatever the reason, if she is half-mad, if he is hurting her—isn't that as bad as anything she's done?"

He turned to the door. "I should rejoin them before he comes looking for me."

I wished he'd send Smollings away. Forever. I never wanted to see his face again. In just a day, I had come to understand why Vestenveld's halls were heavy, and why Hollin felt his father's spirit still lingered, protecting his taxidermy. The true master of Hollin's home had arrived.

12

The next morning, Erris began to spell furiously the moment I wound him up. THAT FIEND!

I knew whom he meant, of course. In his world, lived in fits and starts, I supposed Smollings had just left the room.

HE INSULTED YOU.

"Well, you're kind to think of me first, but that's the least of our worries." Still, his words vanquished some of the humiliation I had felt. I wondered if I should tell Erris what Smollings had said after he had wound down, about destroying him. I didn't want to distress him when he couldn't fight back.

SMOLLINGS . . . Erris made a growling sound in his throat. TOUCHED ME. His hands jerked wildly, the closest he could come to thrashing. I briefly draped my hand over his, and he stilled.

"He suspects you're alive," I said. "He implied, in fact . . . that you might be a . . . a long-lost fairy prince."

"*Mmm.*" His grunt had the inflection of a well-chosen curse word. YES, he spelled.

"You're the heir to the throne?"

NO, he spelled quickly. His fingers lurched back and forth between the two letters. NO NO NO.

"I'm sorry," I said. "I just thought— Well, Smollings said people had been looking for you."

IMPOSSIBLE. NINTH SON. NOT KING.

"But you are a prince, then?"

YES.

Smollings had made it sound as if the whole family had been killed, save the missing son. Perhaps Erris didn't even know. If this was the case, I had no wish to convey the news. Especially not when he was still trapped like this, unable to pace, to rage, to cry.

An unwanted thought pushed its way forward as I considered the tangles of Erris's life—or lack thereof. "Erris, do you have a body? Did they turn your body into an automaton somehow? Or is your body dead? Are you a ghost?"

Erris's eyes rose to mine, and even in his expressionless face, I thought I saw a glimmer of despair. DON'T KNOW.

"Do you know how Garvin meant to free you?"

NO.

I barely took in his last word. The door shot open. No warning. Smollings.

Erris began to play immediately, but I had been caught leaning on his instrument, and I knew shock had flashed on my face before I could hide it.

"Miss Nimira," Smollings said. "Good morning."

"Good morning, Mr. Smollings." I pulled out a miraculous composure, but even my toes were clenched inside my shoes. He must have snuck up on us on purpose. I should have heard the footsteps coming.

"Hollin asked that I give the automaton a more thorough examination, if you don't mind." He stepped closer to me, and so I stepped away. Erris's fingers poked at the keys, playing one of his more melancholy tunes.

Smollings watched Erris's hands; waiting, it seemed, for a mistake. He tucked his arms behind his back, leaning forward to peer closely at the rise and fall of Erris's chest. He watched Erris's eyes make their usual rounds of peering to the side and out at the nonexistent audience. I wondered if it was hard for Erris not to react, or if he could merely allow the clockwork body's mechanism to run its course.

Thinking of this, I reminded myself what an impossible situation we faced. Sometimes, as we spoke in our fashion, I almost forgot the connection between the clockwork body, with its drums and cogs, and the words that came to me through the keys. But surely Erris had no living body to return to. If Garvin had been unable to help him, what could Karstor do? Did any sorcerer on earth have the power to give life to someone without a living body?

Necromancers could raise the dead, but it was not a natural life. Undeath, they called it in Lorinar. In Tiansher, we called those who lived this way walking corpses, and considered them cursed. The most unsavory necromancers would steal bodies. We cremated our dead just so such a thing could not be done.

Maybe Garvin had never intended to help Erris reclaim his

throne, but only wished to tell the world about his fate. Maybe when Garvin said Karstor could help Erris, he meant only that Karstor could show him the way to a peaceful final death.

"Very lifelike," Smollings said, turning to me again. "And you're quite sure you've never seen it do anything unusual?"

"No, sir. He plays and moves the same each time."

"Considering he is nothing but a clockwork toy, you certainly have a lot to say to him."

I knew then he'd heard me talking with Erris. He might have been listening at the door for our entire conversation. I only hoped he couldn't make out my softly spoken words. I knew outright denial would sound as guilty as anything, so I skipped around the subject. "Mr. Smollings, you embarrass me! It's true, I'm lonely in this great big house. I chat with the automaton as one might to a pet ... or a doll."

Smollings reached into his pocket and brought out a shiny ten-piece, a month's salary for a housemaid—or a trouser girl. "I don't suppose this would loosen your tongue?"

"There's nothing to loosen," I said, but then I wondered if my defiance made me look more guilty. I stared at the coin. "I—I do wish I had something to tell you ... When I first came, I almost wished it would come alive. It looks so real. But it hasn't." I looked sadly down at my shoes.

"Well ..." Smollings pocketed the coin. "I know women have soft hearts. I suppose even an enchanted automaton might be very charming. Whatever may happen, I hope you're aware that he is inhuman. And if he is the prince, God help us. I imagine the fairies would kill us all if given half a chance. I know I should not like to think myself responsible for another war because I fancied my enemy to be a pretty little doll to have tea parties with."

He handed me a penny. "Here, girl. A little something for your time. Be sure to let me know if you see anything."

I shoved the coin in my pocket, unable to hide the venom in my eyes entirely, but I kept my lips shut.

13

The next morning, Linza wore a slight smile as she brought my breakfast. "He's gone, miss," she said, when I offered a tentative smile in return.

"Oh, thank goodness." I went limp in my chair.

"He rarely stays long, but days seem like weeks with Smollings around, don't they?" Linza poured me a cup of tea. "We can all breathe easy now."

"Did you see the witch he brought with him?" I asked. "The criminal?"

Her body stiffened. "Witch?"

"Yes, a girl with these orbs floating around her head ran into my room in the middle of the night, begging for help. Smollings dragged her away. He had this staff that was hurting her and she cried out, and Hollin said she was a witch, a madwoman, that Smollings was taking to prison, but it was all very strange."

Spots of pink appeared on Linza's thin cheeks. "That is strange," she said. "But—but it doesn't surprise me. Smollings was chief of the border police when he was younger, I've heard. I'd guess he knows about criminals."

"Linza, do you know something about it? You're flushed."

She quickly shook her head. A bad liar, Linza was, and I was about to tell her so when her eyes welled with tears. When I opened my mouth, she rushed from the room.

I couldn't find her anywhere, so I wandered outside among the sun-baked grasses of the field, gathering the tiny yellow flowers and sprigs of white that swayed in the breeze. I thought to take Erris a bouquet; he'd surely love to see them. He must miss flowers. I twirled daisies between my fingers and played a game I'd read about in a book—does he love me, does he not? I didn't specify who "he" was . . . but he loved me.

IS HE GONE? Erris asked, after I arranged the flowers in a vase atop his pianoforte.

"Yes. This morning."

DID HE HURT YOU?

"What? No. Not really. He tried to bribe me to tell him you'd spoken to me. And he said something about you being a doll I have tea parties with." I made a scoffing sound, but the words stung. Smollings thought no more of me than he would a dust mote. I should have been happy he didn't consider me much threat, but I knew many people of Lorinar shared his view. I had come a long way from my childhood world, where my mother was one of the most admired women at court.

"I should have never left Tiansher. If Mother's looking down on me, she'd say I should have stayed on the farm with Uncle San-cham. I've done nothing but make a mockery of myself since I came."

He made a sympathetic sound. SIT.

I knelt on my knees by the piano bench, keeping his hands just barely in view. "I'm sorry, Erris. I don't even feel like talking."

"Mmm?" he prodded with his tone.

"Oh, it's just . . . I don't know. My mother was so beautiful, so skilled. When she danced, the whole court watched her. She thought I'd follow in her footsteps, but instead I'm here. My home seems like something I imagined rather than a real place half the time, and I've grown used to being called a 'trouser girl' and worse. I don't know how to explain it. I don't know who I am anymore." I swallowed.

YOU ARE JUST NIM TO ME. I LIKE NIM.

"I guess you would know how it feels, if anyone does." Erris was far from home . . . and far from the person he had once been. I wished, how I wished . . . he could take my hand and murmur words of solace in my ear.

The thought was a whisper, forbidden even within the halls of my own mind.

I finally climbed onto the piano bench and sat beside him. I studied him, as I had so many times done. I took a flower from the vase and twirled it between my fingers. I touched the petals to his cheek.

He looked at his hands. His chest rose and fell.

He spelled my name slowly. N-I-M.

I brought the flower back, now sliding the petals along the palm of my hand. "I'm sorry, Erris. I don't mean to make you miss—"

YOU KNOW . . . He paused long. I THINK I AM DEAD.

I let my hand drop to my lap. "You're *not* dead. If you were dead, you wouldn't be here."

YOU ASKED, AM I A GHOST? NEVER WANTED TO ADMIT. PERHAPS . . . I AM. MY REAL BODY MUST BE DEAD.

"But, Karstor . . ."

I didn't finish the sentence, and he didn't volunteer anything for me.

"Erris, I can't accept— I mean, if you are a ghost, and if you can't be—*saved* . . . No. No, I won't accept it. You can't possibly have waited all this time, just to die. I was meant to find you, I'm sure of it. I will do anything to save you."

Every person has a reason to walk the earth, Mother always said. Sometimes the path leads in strange directions. An easy thing for her to say, it seemed to me now, when she married and became a dancer, just as she always expected.

Still, if I had a purpose, surely it must be to save Erris, and even Hollin himself. I had come to Lorinar to seek my fortune, but in three years, I had found nothing like a fortune. I might as well have stayed in Tiansher if my life was to be an endless round of seedy halls and pennies for pay, watching the songs of my country lose their potency as they touched indifferent ears. This was my chance to be something more, my chance to act.

If I ever had the chance. I didn't have the liberty to jaunt off and hunt down Karstor.

I THINK I MIGHT BE BEYOND SAVING.

"Hush. Hush!" I cried, as if his words were spoken. I shot up from the bench, furious—at Erris, or at myself, I couldn't yet tell. "Don't talk like that—I won't look at you if you do. There must be something I can do. There's something, or Garvin would have told you it was helpless. If I don't save you, this is all worthless. My whole life is worthless." I shuddered and wrapped my arms around myself.

"Mmm," he begged. "Mmm!"

"Please don't." I kept my face turned away from him a little longer, and then my resolve broke.

"Mmm." He wanted me to come back to his side. I sunk down again, beside him, and put my forehead to his shoulder. Beneath his jacket, no life, no warmth, only the ridges of metal parts.

I couldn't bear it.

PLEASE . . . DON'T CRY.

I swiped my hand across my cheek. How could I cry before him, when tears were lost to him? How could I even complain when at least my body was free?

DON'T DESPAIR YET. TALK TO KARSTOR.

"Yes . . ."

WE MUST PRACTICE THESE GHASTLY SONGS. I AM NOT SO DEAD AS TO AVOID THAT.

"No." I wiped my eyes and tried to smile.

"Mmm," he said gently, and he began to play.

14

I had not seen Linza since that morning, so I was surprised when she came to braid my hair for bed, as if nothing had happened.

Well, not quite as if nothing had happened. Her hands trembled as they formed the plait. I burned to ask her questions, but pushing her would do no good. I couldn't force answers from her any more than Smollings could force them from me, and I didn't fancy bribery.

"There. All ready," Linza whispered, letting my braids fall against my back. Then, "Miss."

"Yes?"

"The—the witch . . . did Mr. Smollings really hurt her? With his staff?"

"Yes."

"She begged for help? What did she say?"

"Not much. Her hands were tied, and she asked me to untie them."

"I wanted to tell you this morning, Miss Nimira," she said. "I'm scared to lose my job, with Mother's rheumatism ... but this isn't right and I ought to tell you." She closed her eyes tight, like she wanted to hide from her own words. "That woman you saw is Mr. Parry's wife."

I exhaled, and reached for the edge of the table. "His wife?"

"Yes, miss."

"But ... she died of a fever. Didn't she?"

"Not exactly, miss. She's not well, but she's not dead, either."

"But he told people she's dead? And he keeps her locked up?"

"*He* doesn't ... exactly."

"Then who does?"

"Mr. Smollings. And Miss Rashten works for him. She makes sure the mistress can't escape—oh, dear, I really shouldn't be telling you all this."

"Is she mad?"

"She's not really mad. Well, she's odd, that's true, but ..."

"Odd how?"

"I'm not sure all of what happened. I'd just started working here when she got sick, but Mr. Parry tried some terrible magic to save her, and something happened. He let something dark get into her. I've heard she can talk to the dead now. Those orbs follow her around. Spirits. And she stays in the dark. Lights make her sick."

"Why is she locked up?"

"On account of the forbidden magic Mr. Parry used to try and save her. I guess he'd go to jail if the council knew, and none of us want that to happen." She added, "Mr. Parry is a good man, miss. He pays us all good wages."

No doubt he does, with that sort of secret, I thought bitterly. He'd told me she was a witch and a madwoman. His own wife. He dined with me, and hinted at a future, while his wife dwelt captive in this very house.

"I'm sorry," Linza said in a hush. "But I thought you should know."

"No one shall ever know you told me," I said. "Thank you."

She hurried from the room.

15

A door blocked off the stairs to the third floor, but no one had locked it, and no one saw me slip through it—I made sure of that. Some furniture cluttered the third-floor halls: a settee with torn upholstery and a dented wardrobe, covered in dust, save four long lines where fingers had raked through the gray.

I crept forward on stocking feet. Some doors were locked tight, with only silence behind them, while others hung open to empty rooms, cleared of all furniture. Only the dark drapes remained, blocking the light and stifling the air. Spiderwebs clung to light fixtures and corners.

A whiff of fresh air drew me to the tower room, above the place where Hollin and I sometimes dined. This room still had furniture, all draped in white sheets. Gauzy curtains billowed in the breeze that slipped through cracked windows, yet even with the sunshine, the loneliness was palpable.

I pulled up the corner of one cloth, revealing the dainty curved leg of a chair. Pink upholstery covered the seat. Very feminine.

I wondered if they had been Annalie's rooms once, and if she had been moved to new quarters. I glanced around at the shrouded forms of chairs and end tables. A red, fringed Karadul rug covered the wooden floor. The wallpaper had faded rectangles where paintings or photographs had once hung. One cloth concealed a vase glazed in a deep green.

The largest piece of furniture rested under the window. I had assumed it was a desk, and sure enough, lifting the cloth revealed an elegant rolltop. Slowly, I lifted the top to see an array of shelves and pigeonholes, with a few things still housed in them—a book, a few sheets of paper, and a pencil with a chewed end. A tiny spider lay on its back, legs curled.

I plucked a sheet of paper from the group. *Mrs. Annalie Swibert Parry*, the letterhead read. I thumbed through the rest, but none had any writing.

I picked up the book. *The Diaries of a Lady Adventurer, penned by Lady Montswire.* I cracked the cover, and a pressed flower slid out onto the desktop. The first page bore an inscription:

To my dearest Annalie—

Soon you will be my own beloved lady adventurer, and the tales we shall tell will put Lady Montswire to shame. Can you imagine—the two of us in the port of Sormesen, dinner on the river &c.? The God's Gate, the floating city, the tombs of Gyntia—it's as if the world was built for us. We'll end with a safari, and we won't leave until you've seen at least one tiger—and no, we won't turn it into gold!

I'll be home soon, but until then, read this book and dream of our future, while I remain,

Your Devoted,
Hollin

I stared at the fine, slanting hand for a long time before I returned the pressed flower to the yellowing pages and clapped the book shut.

I moved on. A copper statue of a woman in a flowing dress guarded the fourth-floor stair. Like everything else, she wore a film of dust. The steps groaned under my feet. I walked close to the edge, where the wood wouldn't bow as much, keeping a light touch on the banister. No dust on the banister. These stairs were still used, then.

On the fourth floor, I passed a number of unremarkable rooms and several more locked doors.

Did I hear something creak?

I froze, looking off down the hall. I heard it again. The stairs. And also, the gentle clattering of silver and china, like the way our dining room table would rattle at Granden's rowhouse when a train went by.

Oh, God, someone was coming.

I dashed through the nearest open door, heart fluttering like a rabbit's, nearly tripping over a stack of books on the floor. A desk faced the window, and shelves lined the rest of the walls, full of tiny stoppered bottles containing strangely colored liquids, crystals, and other trappings of sorcery, and books—great musty tomes with strange letters on their spines, with gold embossing, with locks on the covers.

"Someone there?" I heard Miss Rashten call, her voice nasty. She drew ever closer.

My eyes swept the room again and again, to no avail. There was no closet or wardrobe to duck into, nowhere to conceal myself.

Miss Rashten stepped through the door, her curls bobbing beneath her cap. She held a silver-covered tray of food—I smelled boiled meat—which she quickly put on the desk. Before I could move, before I could speak, she set upon me. She struck my arm so hard that I gasped with pain. Then she grabbed me, her fingers bruising, and yanked me from the room.

"What are you *doing*?" She spoke close to my ear.

"I— I—"

Miss Rashten pulled shut the door and locked it. "You *answer* me: why were you up here where Master Parry told you not to be?"

"I—"

"You were looking for something."

"I just wondered what was up here. I heard a strange noise."

"Likely it was the sound of your common sense dashing off," Miss Rashten snapped. "You need to keep from poking around. Do as you're told."

"I was afraid it could have been a ghost."

"No ghosts in this house. If you want to stay here, you'll keep quiet and behave yourself. And you never, ever mention anything you may have seen or heard up here, or I will tell Master Smollings and you'll reckon with him. You understand me quite clearly?"

"Yes'm." I fidgeted. I felt utterly foolish for getting caught, but it was best if Miss Rashten thought me a fool as well.

"You will not come up here again?"

"No."

"The consequences for trespassing next time will be far, far more severe." She pointed at the stairs. "Go on with you."

16

If I seemed preoccupied when I spoke to Hollin, if I shied back when he gave me a compliment, he never called attention to it. I suspected that Smollings's visit had ruffled him as much as me, although I might not understand all his reasons.

It was wrong for Hollin to lie about his wife, no doubt of that. But I wondered if Hollin might be as much a prisoner as she was. Linza said he had used illegal magic to save her life, the action of a desperate man, not a villain. If Hollin could stand up to Smollings . . . Surely it wasn't too late to set things right.

I dreaded the performance at Aldren Hall. Hollin told me that the guests would be Lorinar's elite, and I must let him take the lead. I imagined a vast house full of people who would laugh at me behind gloved hands, and somewhere in the midst of it all I had to find Karstor, a man I had never met, and warn him of Smollings's plan. The day arrived all too soon. Hollin appeared in the doorway with Linza at his heels.

"Mr. Smollings requested you wear your trousers to Aldren Hall," he said.

"I thought you had the gown made for my performances!" I didn't want to appear as Smollings wished, encouraging those rich ladies and gentlemen to gawk.

He frowned. "Well, what am I to tell him?"

"Tell him I have a gown."

"But you also have trousers." He nodded for Linza to proceed, while he turned from the door.

Linza gave me a weak smile. Perhaps she feared what I might say with temper rising on my face. "You will look lovely in your mother's clothes," she said.

I sighed and flung open my trunk.

She helped me tie the embroidered sash behind my back, over the dancing tunic with the shawl collar that barely touched my shoulders, and "trousers" that buttoned just below my knees like knickers. I let my braids down, and atop my head she placed the only jewelry I had taken from home, a gold-plate circlet of little value. A fan of stiff wire draped with beads rose from the back of it.

"I pin it like this?"

"That's right. A few pins in back and it will stay."

I lifted my dark eyes to my mother's reflection. Oh, I had Aunt Vinya's nose, of course, but so many vague memories of my mother now sharpened, seeing myself as she had been. I recalled how she would sit in front of the mirror and run color across her lips with a fingertip, how she would let me paw through her jewelry and drape extra bangles on my skinny little-girl arms.

"Are you all right, Miss Nimira? You look like you haven't slept."

"I haven't."

We exchanged sympathetic expressions in the mirror, but I couldn't think what more to say.

I wished I could confide in her. I wished I could say that I didn't want to stand up in front of a crowd in my strange trousers, that I hardly knew who I was anymore, that my mother would be sorely disappointed in me, that Hollin wanted things from me that I wasn't sure I could give, that I feared I had feelings for Erris I should never have felt, that I would fail to save him. I craved understanding, a gentle touch to my shoulder, a kind word.

Yet, some terrible pride seized my tongue. I had always been the strong one. I had always been "above" things. If I cried, I cried alone.

"I think I just have a touch of stage fright."

A heavy tread came to a stop in the doorway. Linza and I both glanced over to see Hollin there.

"How do I look?" I stood up and pulled my tunic straight, frowning at a wrinkle near the hem.

"Nimira, you're right. Change into the evening gown."

His abrupt decision left me startled. "The gown?"

"Smollings won't be able to do a damn thing about it once we're all there. I want them to see you as the well-spoken traveler you are, not an imported curiosity." He slapped the doorframe before he turned away.

Linza raised her eyebrows. "The gown it is, then."

She brought forth the splendid gown, with its rustling silk and air of grandeur. It dipped low in back and front, with cream and black velvet flowers crawling around the neckline, exposing what seemed like far too much of my brown skin. I tried not to care how pale Linza's hands were against mine. The bodice hugged my form and the skirts swept around my legs, so different from the clothes of Tiansher, meant for moving and stretching and leaping.

Linza dressed my hair in a pompadour and pinned velvet flowers that matched the flowers on my gown just above my ears. She spritzed my hair and neck with some scented water until I smelled like a spring garden. Finally, she handed me my long ivory gloves, waited as I tugged each finger straight, and draped my cape around my shoulders.

Hollin watched me descend the stairs. He looked quite serious. I tried to smile.

"You are a queen of Shai," he said, referring to the long-gone country Tiansher had once been a state of, a land I had noticed stories of Lorinar tended to romanticize.

"I would have been a queen of Shai if I'd worn the trousers. But I'm glad you changed your mind."

He offered me his hand as I took the bottom step. "One more touch, I think." He took something from his pocket—diamonds gleamed in the light. His hands slipped around my neck. It wasn't just the corset that restrained my breath as he fastened it. His hands lingered on my shoulders an extra moment before he removed them.

"I meant to give Annalie this necklace on her birthday," he said. "But I never got the chance."

I touched the gems. The platinum settings felt cold and weighty on my skin. I could imagine him giving them to his smiling bride, and the thought stabbed at me.

He swallowed, looking strangely forlorn as he studied the way the diamonds rested. "You—you look very beautiful tonight, Nimira."

Despite it all, I thought of touching his cheeks—of warming the skin there. "Thank you, sir."

"Shall I escort you to your carriage?" He held up his arm.

I slipped my gloved hand into the crook of his elbow.

⟐

Aldren Hall was a smaller estate than Vestenveld, probably built in the last century, if I could judge by the illustrations in novels. Their bewigged romantic heroes always had estates like this: a broad rectangle of stone with two extended wings branching off the sides. Three rows of windows glittered with light from one wing to the other. A line of carriages looped around the curving driveway, dropping their guests off at the door before trotting on.

As we approached the doors, Hollin took my arm again. I suppressed a grin of pride. I would enter in a gown, on a man's arm, like a lady.

We were received in a grand hall, under a glittering chandelier. The servants taking our wraps and hats wore curled white wigs, black uniforms trimmed in gold, and white stockings. All around us, gentlemen removed their top hats; ladies shed their shawls and capes to reveal creamy shoulders. Jewels of every color and staggering size hung around their necks, and I was glad I had the diamonds. Annalie's diamonds. I never forgot their presence. Cheerful chatter echoed across the wooden floors, mingled with the whispering of delicate slippers, the rustling of dresses, the firm clattering of male dress shoes.

The crowds spilled forward into the hall, where marble statues perched at the foot of the floating staircase. They had little wings and carried spears, so I supposed them some manner of mythical creature. Portraits lined the walls, rosy-cheeked girls in massive gilt frames that were works of art in themselves. On the second floor, a girl chased a fellow up the stairs; their laughter floated over the crowd. A strange smell hovered in the air, an alluring smoke I almost thought I recognized from childhood.

An older woman spotted us across the room and hurried our way.

"Mr. Parry! Oh, this must be the girl I've heard of, the lovely maiden of Tassim."

"Lady Moseky." Hollin regarded her with a slight bow.

Lady Moseky had a lively, lined face with deep-set brown eyes. Her eyebrows were nearly nonexistent, enhanced with pencil. "I've placed your automaton in the drawing room—what an amazing piece! If you ever wish to sell, do let me know."

"That I will."

"Brilliant." She moved along, searching the crowd, the beading on her black dress shimmering.

"She is the hostess?" I asked.

"Yes. Very eccentric woman, but also very rich." Hollin wore a look of distaste as he spoke. "Her father was the ambassador of magic for a time when I was a boy. Sorcerers and politicians have always gathered here, but since her father died ten years ago, she has let in more and more of an . . . unsuitable crowd. The radicals and reformists." His voice dropped. "And speak of the devil."

"Good evening, Mr. Parry." A man stepped into our conversation, dressed all in black with a blue cravat, a sardonic smile already on his lips. "I heard you'll be providing some entertainment for us this evening." He had a foreign accent—a slight heaviness to certain syllables, a sharpness to his *r*'s.

"Yes. This is Nimira." Hollin was looking ahead, as if he hoped to spot a friend in the crowd who might pull him away.

"She is the singer, yes? To accompany . . . an automaton?"

Hollin nodded vaguely. His arm was stiff under my fingers. "Oh, I beg your pardon, there's Melsing, I'd better say hello." He began to move on, bringing me with him through the press of crowds.

I glanced back at the man as Hollin led away, and was startled to see him watching us depart. I quickly faced forward. "Who was that?"

"Karstor Greinfern."

Karstor! My God, that was *Karstor*? I feigned nonchalance. "What's wrong? I'd think you'd want to talk to him after that plan you and Smollings—"

"Shh!" he snapped, although with so many people talking all at once, I doubted anyone could hear. He wouldn't meet my eyes. "Karstor is dangerous. He and Garvin were full of disastrous ideas . . ." Hollin shook his head. "Let Smollings talk to him."

"Disastrous ideas? Like the fairy alliance?"

"Precisely."

"Smollings thinks an alliance will lead to war, then?"

"He thinks they'll betray us."

"What will happen if there is no alliance? Peace?"

"You need not concern yourself."

I put my hand to his arm. "Stop saying that, Hollin, please. This is my country now, and I want to know if there will be war. War isn't just a business for men, you know. It affects everyone."

He paused. "I don't know if war is inevitable, but Smollings wants to assure us the upper hand, whatever the outcome."

Was the war inevitable? If Erris was the lost prince, and if Garvin, as the ambassador of magic, had meant to save his life and restore his throne, then I could hardly imagine our two countries going to war. But if Erris couldn't be saved ... then what had Garvin's plan been?

I needed to talk to Karstor.

All around us, people laughed and talked. Ladies' bare arms and gentlemen's sleeves brushed us in the thick crowd. Hollin found us breathing room in the airy ballroom, a space twice as long as it was wide, and full of waltzing couples. Chairs lined the paneled walls, many of them occupied by ladies fanning themselves or chatting while their eyes followed the dancers. I saw more of the eccentric company Hollin had mentioned; dandies wearing velvet knickers and their hair long, and a girl with a small monkey clinging to her shoulder.

Hollin drew me just to the side of the doors. "That's better. Much too crowded in the hall."

"Yes." Dancing partners whirled by us, their feet moving together, although some kept better time than others. I watched one clumsy pair near my age, both blushing.

Of course, I expected Hollin to ask me to dance. I didn't know what to do when he merely stood there, brooding upon the couples sweeping by. "Do you like to dance?" I asked him.

"Not very much, not anymore."

"Did you dance with Annalie?"

"Well, Anni, she was not the most coordinated of girls. Despite all her lessons, she was always, well, a rather terrible dancer." He smiled faintly, and then it was gone. "Do you know the waltz, Nimira?"

"I do, yes." Polly had taught me and Saraki both the social

dances of Lorinar. I didn't mention that. Dancing had been one of the evening amusements at Granden's, with Eila taking the piano.

"One dance, I suppose . . ." He tilted his head toward the floor. "If you'd like to, that is."

"Yes, all right."

He led me onto the floor, and we took our positions. We had only a moment to get our hands and feet in the right place; the couples were whirling around the floor in a slow circle, and we had to fall in with them or collide. Before I knew it, I was in Hollin's arms, slowly spinning. I took my skirt up with one hand after I nearly stumbled on the hem.

He cut a fine figure on the floor, and I could not help thinking what an attractive couple we must make. When I danced, I felt light. I could have closed my eyes and imagined another life, where I loved the arms that encircled me. I wanted to toss my burdens aside and never take them up again.

When I looked up, his face was distant and serious. He made a halfhearted smile before I lost him again. I wondered if he was thinking of Annalie. Or was he brooding over Karstor and fairy alliances? Or looking for Smollings? Too many possibilities, none of them good.

"You should smile more." I spoke into his ear over the music. "It becomes you."

His cheeks flushed, and his true smile came out. "Does it, now? I'll try to remember. I do want to keep my Nimira happy, or else you might step on my toes."

My Nimira!

I wanted to jerk back from his arms. Surely he didn't think of me as his, just because of a few shared meals and conversations? He was a married man. Maybe Annalie was a bit mad, maybe he no longer loved her, but that didn't make it right to woo me, especially if he was keeping the truth from me.

But Hollin also owned the clockwork body of Erris. If I rebuffed him and he sent me away, I'd have no chance of saving Erris. I kept dancing, kept smiling. It was a good thing I knew how to pretend.

The music ended, and we saw Smollings break away from a man he'd been speaking with near the doors and head our way. A merry polka was starting up, but Hollin led me off the floor. His smile had vanished.

"Good evening, Hollin. Nimira. Where exactly is your costume for the performance?" We stopped in one corner of the dance floor.

"I changed my mind," Hollin said, quite firmly. I squeezed his hand. *Yes—hold your ground!* "I had already bought Nimira this dress."

"You can dress her however you like; it won't change what she is," Smollings said. He shooed me with a thin hand. "Why don't you go say hello to Lady Moseky, she rather enjoys ... your kind. Hollin and I have some business to discuss, hey?"

Hollin released my hand, and for a moment he blazed at Smollings in dreadful silence.

"Oh, cool your temper," Smollings said. "You're just like your father. Come on."

"Fine," Hollin snapped. He stalked past Smollings to the door.

"Karstor is here," I heard Smollings say, before they disappeared through the increasing throngs of ballroom spectators. I stepped aside, unsure where to go. I wanted to find Karstor, but I didn't want Smollings to catch us speaking. He'd be distracted talking to Hollin now, but I had to be careful.

It was no easy task to find anyone in such a crowd. If a curtain caught fire we'd all die in the stampede. I skirted the edge of the ballroom, scanning the faces for Karstor's, begging people's pardon a dozen times as I nudged past them, heading for the double doors at the other end of the room.

I didn't know where they'd lead, but I hardly cared. I needed air. I brushed past two men in a heated discussion, one of them gesturing with a closed lady's fan, as if he'd forgotten he were holding it. The dancers were lost in their own worlds. A little boy and girl were hiding under a table, whispering to each other, passing a pastry back and forth.

I darted behind the doors, into a large room lit by just one dim lantern on the table and moonlight streaming in through the windows.

I wasn't alone.

Erris and his pianoforte sat at one end, awaiting the crowds that would come after dinner to see him play. To see me sing.

I approached him like I might step into a tomb. It wasn't right that he should be here, shut away with only a feeble light for company, unwound and silent, while just behind the doors was dancing and laughter. Erris liked dancing, I suspected. He must know a number of interesting fairy dances.

I wanted to wind him, but I didn't have his key. It would be foolish, anyway. I touched his arm, and brushed the hair off his face. It flopped right back into place.

I should talk to Karstor, I must. But my reluctance ran deeper than my fear of Smollings. If Karstor couldn't save Erris, I couldn't bear to hear it. I didn't want Erris to die.

Nim, you must do something. One way or another, you can't leave him trapped in an automaton. Everyone must die sooner or later, and he has no life to speak of.

"Karstor's here," I said aloud, as if he could hear me. "I'm sorry I haven't spoken to him yet, but I will. I haven't had a chance."

I looked at his hands, an automatic reaction by now. Of course, they remained still. A clock on the mantel ticked a slow time, the sound heavy over the sprightly music that floated through the doors.

I pressed my lips together.

Even if Erris couldn't speak, a voice in my head readily spoke for him. *Nim, you know you must talk to Karstor. Hollin is occupied. It may be your only chance.*

"I will," I repeated, as if it helped. I squeezed his cold hand, wishing I could feel the life inside him.

I cracked the door and peered out to the ballroom again. I scanned the walls, where people spoke in small groups, laughing and gesturing. Finally, I spotted Karstor halfway between the other entrance and myself, speaking to a woman, and then to her friend. One of them noticed me and pointed. Karstor caught my eye and nodded.

Startled, I ducked back inside the quiet room. Karstor was asking after me? I hoped Smollings didn't catch wind of *that*.

He opened the door. "Might I talk with you a moment?"

"Um . . . yes. Why?"

As soon as he shut the door behind him, his attention shifted to Erris. "The automaton." He spoke softly. "I have never seen it. I was abroad when Garvin—"

My stomach clenched as he walked close.

"He's beautiful." Karstor ran his hand along the pianoforte. He had long hands, stained with ink around the writing fingers. "I suppose you have heard that he is haunted?"

"I've heard that." I wondered how much Karstor knew, what Garvin might have told him. He was handling me carefully, I guessed. He didn't know if he could trust me either.

"Do you believe it?" he continued.

If I was to tell him, it was now or never. I spoke in a rush. "He's not haunted, sir. He's alive. He told me to talk to you. But we don't have much time. Smollings mustn't see us. He suspects."

Karstor drew close enough to touch me, something like panic on his gaunt face. His smell reminded me of anise—somewhere between baked goods and medicine. "So he *has* talked to you. And you know what—who—he is? Do you have his key?"

"I know he's . . . a fairy prince. I'm afraid I don't have his key. Not here."

"What else has he said? Anything about Garvin?"

"Well, sir, he said he didn't think fairy bandits murdered him."

"Does he know who did?"

"No . . . he only suspected it was Garvin's human rivals."

"The automaton might have been the last person to talk to Garvin. I had hoped he knew something . . ." He scratched the side of his forehead, with the weariest of expressions.

"Do you know how to set him free? Erris—the automaton—he told me to ask you. Garvin had been trying to help him before he . . ."

Karstor stopped short, looking at Erris. "How to set him free? How do you mean, free?"

"I mean—" My fingers tugged at Annalie's diamonds. "I mean, is there a way he can live again? He's trapped. Garvin said you could help."

"Is that what Garvin told him?" He shook his head. "Garvin

was ever the optimist. I told him I can't make life from clockwork. I can only raise the dead. But I'd need a body, his body—and the council's permission."

Nim, you expected this. You expected this. Don't you dare cry. He will not see you cry, some stranger who is no help at all . . .

I blinked rapidly, fighting off the tears. "But what was his purpose, then? Garvin wasn't going to help restore him to the throne?"

"Well . . . this is something we were trying to figure out, before Garvin's . . . death. He certainly is not without uses. There are some in the fairy realm who would like to have him back, others who would not. We could bargain, or offer him as a gift of goodwill . . ."

"Offer him as a *gift*? And then what?" Now the tears crept into my voice, and I was in peril of losing my control entirely. "Can *they* save him?"

"I—I don't know. Only the Lady could grant—perhaps—"

I lifted my head.

Perhaps there was a chance, then. "The Lady? Who is that?"

"She goes by many names. The Queen of the Longest Night. The Queen of the Dead. Those of us who commune with the other side have felt her touch, and she is not unkind, but . . . it is dangerous to attempt such magic. Opening the gates of the dead as wide as that would invite many evil spirits in. Very dangerous. And illegal, without the council's permission."

"You said you'd need a body. Does he have . . . a body somewhere?" I couldn't believe I would actually suggest this. Undeath, that great taboo, for Erris. He could not have meant *that* when he asked for life, so why did I ask?

Against all sense, I still wanted to know what Karstor could do. I heard tales of undead men who could not be distinguished from living ones. They had always made me shiver, but now I wondered—if I could grant Erris just a day, a week, a month—only to have a proper good-bye, I told myself . . . I did not dream of having any more than that.

Karstor smiled without humor. "It has been too long. Nearly thirty years. I think his body, if it could even be found, would be rather past the point of help."

"I know," I said quickly. My heart thumped too fast, as if reminding me of my own life. "No more. I understand." I should not even speak of these things.

Outside, I realized the last waltz had ended and nothing had replaced it. "Oh, the music stopped. Why did the music stop?"

"It must be time for dinner."

The door burst open, and I whirled with fear. A girl's face poked in. "Oh! Sorry to scare you!" she said. "I'm looking for my brother!" The door shut again, leaving me with knees like pudding.

"If you go out to the ballroom, I'll go out the other door and slip in from the main hall," Karstor said.

As I left, I saw him put his hand on Erris's arm, with all the gentleness Smollings had lacked.

17

I fell in with a crowd leaving the ballroom. My eyes felt swollen with tears waiting to be shed, but when I caught a glimpse of myself in a mirror, all was well upon my face, if not in my heart. The servants were pulling out chairs to convert the room into a dining hall large enough for the many guests. I found Hollin past the main hall, sulking in the little cave of bookshelves tucked under the stairwell.

"How did it go with Mr. Smollings?" I asked.

"Fine," Hollin said. "I suppose we won't know what becomes of his plan until we see how Karstor reacts to the automaton."

Oh, no. I realized that, among all my other concerns, I had forgotten to warn Karstor not to react to Erris's appearance and certainly not to confirm that he was the prince. Did I dare speak to him again? My eyes darted beyond Hollin before I could think better of it.

"Nimira . . ." He sounded ragged. He reached for the tips of my fingers. "Smollings thinks I ought to send you away. He asked me why I hired you in the first place. I thought I wanted a singer, but maybe it's—maybe it's company I wanted, all along."

His dark eyes were so intense, just like that first time, across the room from the stage. How long had it been? I counted the days. Not yet three weeks. It felt like an eternity.

"It is . . . ? Well—" I could ask, *You don't want me to sing, then?* I feared the response.

Hollin let go of my hand. He peered out from the bookshelf like he had heard someone, but no one came. He turned back to me, his eyes traveling to my neck, and I realized I had been fidgeting with Annalie's diamonds again.

"We won't talk about this now," he said. He held out his arm. "Come on."

I wished I had said something more, only I didn't know quite what it would have been.

We dined on tiny stuffed birds; I ate just enough to stave off hunger. I tried to listen to conversation about people I didn't know, plays I'd never seen, and places I'd never been to, but my inner voice was loudest.

What is he implying?

Don't be so shocked, Nim. He's hinted at affection for you from the start.

But he has a wife whom he allows to be locked up. And you don't love him. What could you say?

What will become of you and Erris alike if you reject his advances?

Maybe you should just tell Hollin that Erris is alive.

Oh, so he can turn right around and tell Smollings?

Hollin didn't speak much at dinner either. Sometimes he glanced at me, too quick for me to look back. Karstor sat at the other end of the table, and I sorely wished I could send him a psychic message, for I saw no way to send him a verbal one.

The dessert course came around. "After this, we'll adjourn to the drawing room, and you will perform," Hollin told me. "Are you ready?"

"Of course." I spoke with confidence, but I wished I could bow out and curl up in the library at Vestenveld, without anyone looking at me.

The servants had brought a number of chairs and sofas into the drawing room, all facing the pianoforte. Hollin and I waited in the corner, behind the instrument, while the party settled themselves. I witnessed social maneuverings in action; the dandies sat together in the back, the eccentric ladies took chairs near the front, Smollings leaned against the back wall with an amused smile. Karstor stood alone, arms crossed, one shoulder propped against a window frame. Both men seemed to hold themselves apart from the rest of the crowd, but only in Karstor did I see loneliness in the dark, tired eyes. I wondered if he also suspected that Smollings might have murdered Garvin.

Hollin conferred with Lady Moseky, then nodded to me. He took Erris's key from his pocket while I moved in front of the pianoforte.

I heard the key grind.

This was wrong, I thought. Dozens upon dozens of faces gazed on Erris as if he were a toy. Only I knew he had to bury his humanity away. He had no control over the songs he would play. He could never even truly see his audience, for his eyes must always give only the same brief glance in the same directions, every time.

He might never live, never speak with a voice. This very well might be all the world could ever give him. All I could give him.

No, I couldn't think of all this now. I must listen for my cue.

I heard the clockwork mechanism clicking along, but no music. Hollin tapped the piano bench with his toe. "This is strange. He isn't playing."

I turned to see Erris still in the same stiff pose. His hands were vibrating a little, nothing more.

Hollin lifted Erris's coat and parted his shirt, where the metallic drum turned slowly around. "My apologies, ladies and gentlemen, just a moment."

To my horror, Karstor stepped forward. "Something must have broken."

"Dr. Greinfern, I wasn't aware you knew anything about automatons," Smollings said, sounding a little sarcastic.

"I have a little experience. My great-uncle was a clockmaker, and in my youth I used to help him build clockwork toys, which he sold in his shop also."

"Well," Smollings said, "see if you can get it to work and we'll proceed." He stepped back and let Karstor have a look, flashing a grin at Hollin.

Was Erris refusing to play? I had not told Erris about Smollings's plan, yet the fact that the drum still turned implied to me that this was no mechanical failure.

After a moment, the crowd lost interest in a lanky necromancer peering into a cabinet and started talking and rearranging themselves. More than a few slipped out the door.

"My apologies, ladies and gentlemen," Hollin said after a while. "Tonight's performance is cancelled. Perhaps next time."

Smollings conferred with Hollin in a low voice.

Karstor tilted his head, poked things with a finger, and made an occasional concerned "Hmmm." Finally he straightened and delivered his consensus. "I'd have to take him back to my house for repairs. It won't take but a day."

"No," Smollings said.

"No?" Karstor repeated. "Mr. Parry? What do you say? It is your automaton, is it not?"

"I'm afraid . . . my answer is the same." Hollin spoke reluctantly. "I'll let you know if I change my mind."

"Hollin won't be keeping the automaton long anyway," Smollings said.

"And why is this?" Karstor asked.

"Because I'm going to destroy it." Smollings gave Karstor a moment to look properly aghast before continuing, "Unless I am persuaded otherwise."

"What are you saying?"

"There is an upcoming council vote on which I'd appreciate your support." Smollings smiled at the appalled expression unfolding on Karstor's face. "If this automaton is what I think it is, I suspect you'll be happy to oblige. We wouldn't want anyone to know what Garvin was up to behind the council's back, would we?"

Karstor took a sharp breath, nostrils flaring. "Soleran, I would rather die than let you blackmail my votes. And if you dare try and kill *me*, my ghost will have nothing better to do than follow you to the ends of the earth."

"Poor man," Smollings said. "A dull life, even in death."

Karstor stared at Smollings for a long moment. His lips, his eyes, his hands were all remarkably cool and still, and this lack of reaction somehow conveyed the great sense of power within him. I would have trembled under such a look, but Smollings sniffed and looked away.

Karstor turned sharply on his heel and stalked from the room.

Smollings murmured, "Well, I'd say that did the trick. The next step, I suppose, is getting this thing to talk. Just leave it alone, and I'll come up to Vestenveld next week. Maybe we could use the girl." He looked at me. "She talks to it, Parry."

"She most certainly does not!" Hollin rushed to my defense so quickly I almost felt guilty. "She would have told me."

"I heard her," Smollings said. "I'd keep a close eye on her if I were you."

"I was talking to myself, really," I said, allowing a quaver in my voice that was hardly forced, but that I hoped Hollin would take for loneliness. I thought he would understand loneliness. "The automaton is just there. I like to pretend he can hear me. I don't have many people to talk to."

"You can . . . always talk to me," Hollin said.

Smollings snorted. "Do you really believe her, Hollin? Trousers are good liars." He dropped the "girl," as Lorinarians did when they insulted women of my race in general.

I was hardly surprised to hear the slur from him, but this did nothing to soften the word.

"Nimira is no liar." Hollin's voice rose. "And you are wearing my patience!"

"Can you really afford to lose patience with me?" Smollings said. He started to leave, stopped and sighed. "I told your father I'd be like a father to you, but I don't think he'd know what to do with you either, right about now."

When Smollings left, Hollin and I stood alone in the room. The other guests had all gone in search of better entertainments. Hollin frowned at the floor. Oftentimes, he seemed much older than his years, but just now he seemed a mere boy, unsure how to rebel.

"You don't like him any better than I do," I said finally. "Why do you let him control you? I know you said he'd help advance your career, but would you even want a career under his thumb?" I touched the arm of his jacket, just the barest brush with the tips of my fingers. "Hollin, can't you tell me? I fear your secrets. I know you have them." I touched the diamonds again. Her name was so close to my lips.

"I should like to forget my secrets myself," he said. "If secrets could burn, I'd be the first to light the match." He licked his lips. "Nimira, I told you I need Smollings's influence to join the Sorcerer's Council someday, but in truth, that isn't the biggest reason. When—my wife was dying—I tried to use forbidden magic to save her. Smollings—he knows. I could face banishment from the sorcerer's ranks or worse if the council found out."

"So he's blackmailing you?" I asked. "He's rather fond of that tactic, isn't he?"

"I could lose everything. Home and reputation alike."

"But do you really want to help him stir conflict with the fairies? I don't think your heart is in it. Are you happy?"

"Happy . . ." He shook his head. "I haven't been happy since the day I tried to save Annalie's life."

I wondered why he didn't just tell me Annalie was alive. What did he hope to gain now, keeping me in the dark? Or was it all part of the hold Smollings had on him?

"What sort of life is Smollings leading you to?"

"He hopes to put me on the council ... as his pawn. Save my reputation, sell my soul, I suppose."

"Is that the best choice you have?"

"I'm beginning to wonder," he said. "Something must be done."

18

In the carriage, we sat across from each other in a heavy silence. The lights of Aldren Hall still blazed; many guests would spend the night. The wheels rattled over the road, leading us out into the surrounding farmland, where the world welcomed the full moon. Nocturnal butterflies with shimmering wings fluttered around the straight rows of strawberry plants. Trees and plants alike glowed an eerie deep blue. Hollin wasn't looking out; he stared at a spot somewhere to the left of me.

"You should look outside. I've never seen so many butterflies." I was desperate to start a conversation on some lighthearted matter.

"Garden fairies," Hollin replied, with a rather disinterested glance.

"Oh. I've never seen them before." *Alive,* I added inwardly.

"Nimira, I've been thinking." He shifted position, leaning closer to me.

"I imagine we've both been thinking."

"No, listen. You're right. I can never be happy as long as Smollings has a hold on me. I have no future here. I was thinking . . . we should just leave."

"Leave?"

"I have money enough to keep us up. We can travel the world. We can see the Floating City and the God's Gate—travel the spice routes—my God, think what a life that would be. It would be such an adventure. We'd never think about all this again."

Everything he said to me, he had once said to Annalie. His words echoed the inscription I'd found in the book he'd given her. "This is . . . this is all very sudden—"

"I don't think it's sudden. I think it was inevitable," he said. "The looks you give, Nim . . . Your eyes tell me to trust you."

How could I accept when his wife still lived! Yet, how could I refuse? "I'm not sure—"

"Love isn't sure," he said, now taking my hands in his. I felt their warmth even through our gloves. "It's frightening. But it's full of possibility. And hope."

Oh, how I agreed! But it was not for Hollin that I hoped, and I couldn't pretend otherwise. "It's just, I'm still young, and . . . and are you sure you really feel this way? You've seen how Smollings looks down on me. He won't be the only one. I don't have anything to offer you." I was blurting out things I thought should be said, but they had nothing to do with my real hesitations.

"What must I say to convince you, Nimira? I asked you the other night what you need to be happy. What is it? I'll do everything in my power to grant it to you. We could go back to Tiansher and start your own dancing troupe—anything."

The thought of Hollin in Tiansher running a dancing troupe almost made me laugh. "No. That isn't it."

"What is it?"

I could say the word and Hollin would take me away from New Sweeling. He would cheer up if he saw the sun rise in the Shai Valley. I could taste mangos again. To say nothing of the world's riches I had never seen—the floating cities where the winged people lived, or the temples of Karadul, with shining minarets, tombs for long-forgotten kings. We could drink coffee in a waterfront café in Sormensen like the heroine of my favorite mystery novel and watch the sailboats on the glittering water.

But even the sweetest mango would taste bitter, knowing I had left Erris in Smollings's hands.

"Do you believe the automaton is really the lost fairy prince?"

Hollin pulled back against the seat. "Why?"

"Don't look so suspicious." I spoke fast, as if I could outrun my sadness. "I've just spent a lot of time with it and I've never seen it do anything strange, but it's a beautiful piece of art. I hate the idea that it could end up torn apart or gathering dust somewhere. And if it is the fairy prince, wouldn't destroying it be murder?"

"It would be . . . assassination. To prevent something even worse from happening."

"Is that what you really want? To be accomplice to an assassination? Is that really the kind of man you are?"

Hollin drove his fingers through his hair, yanking the roots. "Nimira, you don't understand—"

"Then help me understand. Explain it to me. If I'm going to go away with you, I need to know you're not the kind of man who would stand by and let an innocent man be killed."

His forehead wrinkled with pain, and he pressed it against the side of the carriage, which could hardly have been comfortable with all the rattling. "My father used to quarrel with Mother over the choices he'd made on the council... He would tell her she was just a woman, she couldn't judge, and he'd give me a certain look and ask me to bring him a glass of brandy. I wanted to please him. But at the same time, I felt a horrid stab of guilt as my mother would rush from the room."

He took a deep breath. "I don't want to be that way. If you can just be a little patient with me. You won't be sorry, Nimira... my darling Nimira. I swear I'll make you happy."

I wanted to tell him that I wasn't his darling. I wanted to take Annalie's diamonds from my neck. But if he sent me away, I'd never have a chance to save Erris.

"Then, before we go...please make sure the automaton is safe."

"Is Smollings right? *Have* you talked to it? Is it alive?"

His suspicion was hard to deny in the intimate confines of the carriage. Maybe the time had come to hint at the truth. "How would I talk to it? It's a machine. It can't talk. But sometimes... I think I feel it. I feel it living, and looking at me. When Smollings first suggested it was alive... I believed him, although I didn't want to. If he is alive... then what a horrible fate, Hollin."

"A horrible fate," he echoed. "Oh, Nimira, you are soft-hearted. I can't do anything to help a fairy prince. If Smollings wants him, he will have him. We can only free ourselves. Please say you'll go. I promise you won't think of it with the fine sea air in your nose and the fine meals on your tongue."

If I agreed, I would have one chance to save Erris. It was more chances than I'd have any other way, it seemed.

It would have to be enough.

19

The next morning, I slept in, sending Linza away when she tried to bring me breakfast. I had no desire to wake. My plan for rescuing Erris would require more luck than I was sure anyone possessed, yet failure was unbearable to ponder.

I finally threw back the covers and dressed alone, twisting my back to reach the buttons. As soon as I laid eyes on Erris that morning I almost started to cry.

Face it, Nimira, this might be the last time. You're no sorceress.

I wound him, wondering if he would now work. The hands immediately began to move.

NIM. I'M SORRY.

"No, Erris. I'm the one who's sorry."

KARSTOR SPOKE TO ME.

"After I left the room? But he doesn't have a key."

MAGIC. LIKE YOU TALK TO A GHOST. HE ASKED ME TO

PRETEND TO BREAK SO HE COULD GET ME HOME, BUT HIS
PLAN FAILED.

"Yes. Yes, I know . . . Well, it's all right." I didn't want to tell him
Karstor's plan had only hastened Smollings's desire to destroy Erris.
"There must be some other way . . ." I stopped talking. My cheer
sounded false. We both knew the state of things.

I KNOW MY FATE. I ONLY WISH I COULD HAVE ONE DAY
WITH YOU. PIANO KEYS DRIVE ME MAD.

"I wish . . . I wish we could have had that, too." I thought I'd add
something like *But I'll always remember you fondly* or *I'm glad I was
able to know you.* That sounded so trite.

"Erris, I don't want to tell you this, but . . . I must. Hollin has
asked me to go away with him." I spoke fast, ignoring Erris's fingers.
"I didn't have much choice. If I said no, I'm sure he'd send me away,
and Smollings might destroy you. So I said yes. It will buy us a little
time and until we leave I will try everything to help you, but if I
fail . . . well, I'm not sure what I can do . . . anymore."

Erris made a low sound in his throat. YOU DON'T LOVE HIM.

"Erris—" I struggled to speak.

I turned away from him. "I think I could. Sometimes I do think
I love him, and then . . ." I faltered. *No,* I wanted to say. *I don't love
him. If there is any direction my heart leans, it is toward you . . .*

ALMOST WISH I'D NEVER KNOWN. SCARED FOR YOU.

I heard footsteps coming—brisk, strong footsteps that certainly didn't belong to a maid. Erris kept his hands in place like he
was still broken, and I quickly moved behind him and lifted his
jacket, pretending to look at his mechanism.

Hollin opened the door. "There you are. Last I heard you were
still sleeping."

"I woke a little while ago." I tapped Erris's piano bench with my toe. "I just wanted to see if he was still broken." My voice had a catch to it, but if Hollin noticed, he didn't show it.

He waved me toward him, but I stayed put. "I have several extra trunks, so if there are any books or things around the house you'd like to take, go and collect them."

Heaven help me, I wasn't ready for this yet! "Sir—are we in such a rush?"

"I don't want Smollings to catch wind of this. No, I want everything packed today and we'll leave first thing tomorrow."

"Tomorrow? But that's too soon!"

I couldn't hide my fear, and Hollin came and placed a hand on my shoulder. "I know it must seem fast, but it's for our happiness. It wouldn't do for Smollings to know I was leaving."

My plan to save Erris seemed more unlikely by the moment, and my fate, all the more real. I was agreeing to run away with a married man! Where did that leave me?

"We'll leave without getting married?" I asked, baiting him yet again to reveal the truth.

"We'll marry on the ship. Plenty of people do."

"You mean, once you have me on the ship you wouldn't have to marry me. There'd be nowhere else for me to go."

My words grew talons in the silence that followed. I should not have sounded so harsh.

"Don't you trust me?" Hollin said.

"It's only, I don't think you understand my position, when I have nothing and you have everything, when your word would always be taken over mine because of your sex, your station, and your nationality. It's not that I don't trust you, but *I* want to be shown respect—to be a *proper* wife. A woman of Lorinar would never run away without getting married!"

He put his hands around my arms and looked straight into my eyes. "Nimira, I swear I will make a proper wife out of you. But if we marry in town, word might get out. The day we set sail, we'll marry, and if you like we can even have a proper wedding in Salcy; I still have family there."

His dark eyes were both sad and hopeful. I saw in them reflections of his thwarted dreams. I did pity him. Annalie was no longer the woman he had married, the woman with whom he had shared all his hopes. If I had loved him, all this might have been different.

"My dear Nimira," he said. "I would never wish to bring you shame."

I lowered my head, reluctant but relenting.

He patted my shoulders. "There, now. No reason to be sad, I know it's overwhelming, but we're setting off on a great adventure. Go and get ready."

I nodded, and turned to pick up the song sheets I'd practiced with, like I meant to bring a few favorites with me. Hollin left in a rush; I supposed he had a lot to do.

As soon as the door shut, I heard Erris's fingers gently tap the piano keys, but I didn't look up. I closed my hand around my throat. Sorrow wedged itself there.

"Mmm. Mmm!" Erris made desperate sounds, and I finally forced myself to read his messages.

DON'T GO. YOU DON'T LOVE HIM!

"Oh, and what am I supposed to do? You can't help me."

CAN'T STAND IT.

I grabbed his hands. Solid as they were, they didn't have much strength to resist me. "Stop it. Stop talking. I can take care of myself. I'll run away if I have to. I have a little money." Very little. Hollin hadn't paid me yet. "I'm doing everything I can!"

"Mm. Mm. Mmmm!" He moaned so loud I worried someone might hear, and finally I released his hands.

NIM. PLEASE.

"You can't help me, Erris. I'm sorry."

He knew it. We had nothing else to say. His clockwork face could show no emotion, but I felt my own limbs tremble, thinking how he must be desperate to move, to rage, to grab me, to stop me, but he couldn't do anything.

Neither of us moved for ten clockwork clicks.

LET US PART ON GOOD TERMS, he finally said.

"Let's not talk of parting yet!" I cried. "I won't give up until I'm on that ship—"

DON'T BLAME YOURSELF FOR FAILING THE IMPOSSIBLE.

"But you didn't think it was impossible at first. Garvin didn't, anyway. He told you to find Karstor, and even Karstor didn't say it was impossible. I don't know how to get you to Karstor, but—"

HUSH, he spelled, his fingers falling soft on the keys. I WON'T SAY GOOD-BYE. I WILL WISH YOU HAPPINESS BEYOND YOUR HOPES.

"You too," I said, and then I thought what a ridiculous thing that was to say to someone in such a position. "We will meet again." Someday. Somewhere. *In the next life . . .*

He bowed his head a little, as he did at the end of a performance.

I looked at him, but his eyes stayed lowered. I knew I must go. This was a good-bye, whether or not we said the word.

I started for the door, and then I dashed back and looked into his eyes. He looked back, and as my eyes blurred with tears, I thought I saw the real man he had once been. The air took substance between us, it pressed on my heart, it tugged at my arms. We could never embrace with our arms, but for that moment, we embraced with our souls.

I leaned in and kissed his rigid lips.

"Mmm," he said, his final word before he wound down, the spark dying from his eyes.

I slid down to the ground and cried.

❧ 20 ❧

I knew those tears must be my last. I wouldn't have a chance to cry again.

Back in my usual quarters, I tried to pack, in case I was left with no choice but to go. I already had my old valise, of course, with Mother's clothes and my old books, but someone had brought a second trunk in during the day and folded my new clothes into it.

Space remained for other books, but I didn't feel like carrying any of Hollin's books with me. I didn't want to take a scrap from Vestenveld, unless I could have brought Erris.

I roamed the halls, sick at heart. I might block my tears, but I couldn't replace them with joy, and hollows filled my soul.

My footsteps brought me to Hollin's father's study. I had not entered that room since I'd taken paper from it, and I hardly knew why I entered it now. I wouldn't be sorry to leave this room behind. The fairies sat waxen on their flowers. I thought of the living ones I had seen, the nocturnal butterflies—how they had glowed and danced over the fields. I wished I could wave my hand and grant them life, and in their dead eyes I saw a reflection of Erris, trapped in clockwork limbs forever.

Hollin's father was dead. There was no reason to keep the fairies here any longer. Hollin should have thrown these things away, and made Vestenveld his own. This room was proof that he didn't even try. He told me he wished to be different, but it was all talk. He wouldn't take action against Smollings even now. He would only run away, where Smollings and Karstor and fairy wars would no longer concern him.

The coward! Had he ever cared?

I shoved the curtains wide. Hollin's father would have had a striking view of Vestenveld's image wavering in the reflection pool. I pulled the window latch, but the frame didn't want to let the window go. With the palm of my hand, I thumped it hard, each time with a great smack. My skin stung. I didn't care if the servants heard me.

The window flew open, and a flower-scented breeze played with a loose lock of my hair.

I took the fairies under glass into my hands. Only the wooden base had any weight. I imagined they'd crumble like dried flowers if I touched them. Horrible dead things.

With a great heave, I pitched them into the reflection pool. They landed in the shallows with just a small splash, and they were gone. Forever.

I stared at the still waters so long that tears came to my eyes. I didn't want to go on a ship with Hollin. I wanted to marry someone I loved. I wanted to free Erris. I wanted to be there the moment it happened—whatever happened.

Even if the only fate left to him was to die, he still deserved that much, not this unnatural imprisonment. And he shouldn't have to die alone. No one should. When Mother died, we had all been there. I had held her hand and felt her grip slacken. I didn't want to hold my mother's hand and watch her die, but I would have felt a thousand times worse if she had died without me.

Karstor had implied that only the Lady, the Queen of the Longest Night, could grant Erris life without a body. Or maybe she could find and revive his body somehow. I didn't know how it would work. Karstor also warned of the danger, but I was growing desperate. I wondered how one summoned her. Did one have to be a necromancer? What would she do if she came?

Karstor said she was not unkind. Back in Tiansher, there was a painting of her in one of the palace halls, where she was smiling and carrying a beacon to lead the dead safely home.

I skimmed Hollin's father's shelf, taking out a book I'd seen before: *Mastery of Man: the Perils of Sorcery and the Summoning of Demons, Illustrated with 32 Color Plates*, by the Reverend Abram Crane.

"The underworld is ruled by a fairy known as the Queen of the Longest Night," the book declared in chapter two. "All sinners, human and fairy alike, fall under the cruel sway of this treacherous creature."

An illustration showed a woman whose scowling face reminded me of the *ukuki*, the trickster spirits of Tiansher. She carried a sword aloft and I suddenly recalled the statue of the sword-bearing woman in the square the day I left New Sweeling. I had thought nothing of the statue that day, but now it seemed a sign.

I read on. The Reverend Abram Crane continued page after page about the damnation that fell upon those who summoned the Queen, and how fickle she was about appearing: "She will only appear to those with the most urgent of needs, the darkest of hearts, the most wicked of souls."

Well, my need was certainly urgent, although I wasn't sure about the rest. I needed a real book on necromancy, one that told me how to work the spell. But as the sun crawled into the treetops, I had not found one, and Hollin summoned me for dinner.

Hollin brought maps to the dinner table, and talked of an itinerary that truly would make world travelers of us.

He was so very happy when he talked of travels or animals or world monuments. "I packed six foreign language books, Nimira. We can practice on the ship; I'm sure we can find other travelers to speak with. That should be fun, I think."

"If I'm not seasick."

"You came across in steerage, I imagine?"

I nodded, wishing to purge the memories of the hundreds of beds, the coughing and crying and snoring of my fellow passengers that kept me awake all night, the food I hardly ate and couldn't keep down, the miserable stink of sweat and fear, some of it my own.

"Bad memories, eh? Steerage isn't fit for dogs. Well, even if you're a little seasick this time around, I'm sure you'll find it more pleasant. In first class we'll have good food, music, and comfortable cabins. And new friends. Travelers are very cosmopolitan people. I'm sure you'll charm them all and hear some fascinating stories. And we can sit on the deck and watch the sunset, or sunrise."

He looked at me hopefully, and when I produced a feeble smile in response, he went on, sounding ever more desperate to cheer me.

"I hope to book us to sail right into Sormesen. They say it's straight out of a fairy tale. The houses are painted bright colors and the sun shines three hundred days a year. A person can scarcely sleep, with all there is to do. I'm looking forward to the galleries ... and the food, they say, is the best in the world, to say nothing of the wine."

Sormesen might have been paradise itself, but I knew I could never be content there.

I still looked for necromancy books after dinner, but I found nothing. It seemed I had no choice but to attempt an even more daring plan. Karstor had said those who speak to the dead would know the Queen.

I had to see Annalie.

21

Linza came to my room that night to dress my hair for bed. She hesitated at my door before she walked over and picked up the brush.

"Are you really going away with Mr. Parry?"

I shifted in my chair to face her, rather than my own wan reflection. "Actually, I wanted to talk to you about that. You trusted me with the secret of Annalie's fate, and now I need to put my trust in you. You know where her room is, don't you?"

"You want to see the mistress? Why?"

I decided it was time to tell Linza the whole story. I thought she would have more sympathy than fear for Erris if she knew what he was, and I was right.

"Poor man!" she gasped. "But what could Mistress Annalie do?"

"I need to know how to summon the Queen of the Longest Night. I don't know if she can tell me, but it's the only chance I have right now."

"Well..." Linza glanced behind her. "Miss Rashten guards Annalie."

"But not all the time," I pointed out. "I see her all over the house."

Linza nodded. "She likes to know everything that goes on."

"When does she sleep?"

"It seems like she never does!" Linza said. "But I believe she sleeps from around midnight to four o'clock, and then takes a rest in the afternoon. Her bedroom is right next to Mistress Annalie's, though, and she has awfully keen hearing." Linza rubbed her own ear, as if recalling a time when Miss Rashten had caught her at something.

"Still, I'm willing to try, if you tell me where her room is. I'll just have to be very quiet."

"I'll take you there, miss," Linza said.

"I don't want to put you in danger."

"I don't want you to get lost up there and stumble into Miss Rashten's room." She grinned. "Besides, Mistress Annalie knows me. She might not let you in without a fuss, and that would surely wake Miss Rashten! I'll come for you at half past midnight."

―――――

Half past midnight came and went, and Linza did not appear. I feared Miss Rashten had caught her skulking in the hall, but maybe she had only fallen asleep. I didn't know how long I should wait for her before I tried to find Annalie myself. I still needed time to summon the Queen, after all.

At one o'clock, I crept upstairs in bare feet and my nightgown. The creaks of my soles on the stairs pierced the stillness, but there was nothing to do but go on.

The third floor was lit by only the faintest shreds of moonlight peering between cracks in the curtains. I waited for my eyes to adjust, and listened, but all was utter silence besides my own soft breath and thumping heart.

When Miss Rashten caught me upstairs before, she had been carrying a tray of food, so when I reached the upstairs library where I had tried to hide from her, I thought Annalie's room must be near. But which door? There were two, both shut. One would be Rashten's room. I pressed my ear to one and heard nothing, but behind the second door, I heard the clatter of plates or dishes.

Linza said Rashten slept at this time, but Annalie liked the dark hours. Dared I risk it? Or could I knock, and see whose voice called? Could I run fast enough if it was Rashten? I glanced down the hall. Likely not. If I eluded her here, she'd catch me on the stairs.

I cursed myself for not asking Linza for directions, just in case, and then I rapped on the door.

I heard a woman's voice call, "Yes?" and I knew. The last time I had heard that voice, she'd been begging for help.

"Mistress Annalie?" I didn't want to spend too much time talking in the hall, lest Miss Rashten hear. I tried the knob, but it was locked.

I heard her footsteps approach. The door swung open, and I stood face-to-face with Hollin's wife.

"Oh!" she said. "Why, come in."

The dim room smelled comfortingly of coffee, and there was light, of the most curious sort. Dozens of glowing orbs hovered in the air like fireflies. A few bobbed around Annalie's head, while others offered gentle illumination to corners. Some flitted by the prisms dangling from the ceiling, scattering soft rainbows across

the floor and furniture. Annalie herself was like a shadow, standing in the center of the room, a straight slender line of girl all clad
in black with loose sleeves, her dark hair flowing past her waist.
Her face was paler even than Linza's.

"It's you," she said. Her ordinary northerner's accent broke
through my shock. "Please, have a seat." She waved a hand at the
slim green sofa, her sleeve fluttering. A few loyal orbs of light followed her every move.

I'd never seen clothes like hers before. She wore no corset, and
her dress was simple, without a single touch of lace or beading. Atop
that she had a long hooded robe, like something a sorceress might
wear in a book. It seemed a lot of clothes to wear in the summer in
a shut-up room, but I realized the air wasn't stuffy as expected. It
had the brisk freshness of an autumn day.

Even with the orbs, I could see only the outlines of the exotic
clutter filling the room: paper fans on the walls, square vases, and
painted screens. The room had more mirrors than I could count in
a glance, reflecting the scant lights. Piles of silk pillows in pink and
yellow would have been quite vibrant in the sun, but here their colors were whispers and shadows. Annalie reached for a silver pot on
a tray in front of us. "Coffee?"

"Oh, no, thank you."

"I love coffee, likely more than I should." She poured herself
a little silver cupful and sipped. "It's still hot." She put it down and
regarded me.

"My servants tell me that my husband is about to run off abroad
with you."

This had to be about the most awkward conversation I'd ever
lived through. "You know about it? You know who I am?"

"There is little I don't know, for what good it does me. If my maids don't tell me, the spirits do." The orbs bobbed around her head, as if nodding agreement.

"I don't really want to leave with him."

"But you agreed. I'm told he's packing all the trunks."

"I only agreed so I'd have a chance to save Erris."

"Erris..." An orb drifted past Annalie's face, and her dark eyes gleamed. "Yes. You need to see Karstor."

"I already saw him, for all the good it did. You know about Erris?"

"Oh, yes. The spirits tell me their secrets." She cocked her head as she spoke, as if she were listening not to her own words, but to uncanny voices floating on the air. "Garvin Pelerine has been to see me."

"Garvin?"

"Yes. He told me about Erris. He says Karstor will know what to do."

I thumped my fist on the couch in frustration. "Well, he didn't! Karstor thinks only the Queen of the Longest Night could save Erris. That's why I came to you. To see if you knew how to summon her."

"The Queen of the Longest Night!" Annalie settled her robe closer around her shoulders. "Very dangerous, yes... but could it work?"

The orbs danced and weaved around her. She watched them thoughtfully.

I was beginning to shiver at the thought of the orbs being actual spirits that she could speak to.

"You talk to Garvin?" I asked.

"I talk to many spirits," she said. "Good ones, bad ones... All the lonely spirits with unfinished business are looking for some-one to hear their stories. They can't move on. Garvin can't rest as long as Erris is trapped and Smollings is free..."

"Is it true, then? Smollings killed Garvin?"

"Yes," Annalie said. "Smollings killed Garvin. He is also the one who keeps me a prisoner here."

"You know Smollings is a murderer?" I cried.

"I know," Annalie said. "But precious little I can do about it when everyone thinks I'm dead or crazy and Hollin doesn't dare stand up to Smollings to tell the world otherwise. Miss Rashten watches everything I do. Believe me, I'd love to see Smollings imprisoned if I could. He plies me with his concoctions so that I can speak to not just *my* spirits, but darker spirits. Sometimes I even see glimpses of the future. Always terrible things. I feel like I really am losing my mind . . . I was coming out of one such trance when I ran into your room that night. I had broken away from him, but not for long, as you can see."

We both paused at the sudden sound of approaching footsteps. Annalie sprung to her feet and rushed to a side door, flinging it open. "If that's Rashten, you must hide! Go under my bed."

The door shut behind me, and darkness closed in so thick that I felt my way to the bed rather than seeing it. I dropped onto my stomach and squeezed myself beneath the bed frame, stifling a shriek as my hand met fur.

I heard a purr in the darkness. Unfortunately, I also heard Miss Rashten's voice. "Yes," she was saying. "I found this one poking around near Nimira's door. She's not in her bed."

"She isn't here," Annalie said, quite calmly. "I don't know why she'd come to me."

"I heard voices."

Annalie laughed. "Voices? Here? Fancy *that*." Then, "Where are you going?"

"I'm checking your bedroom."

The door flung open. I stayed very still and held my breath, but the traitorous cat had other ideas. It suddenly bit my hand, and when I tried to swat it back, it clamped on and began kicking my arm like it was an unfortunate rodent. I could see Miss Rashten's feet draw nearer as I grabbed the cat by its scruff and detached it from my injured flesh.

The cat twisted and tore out from under the bed with a low growl. Miss Rashten shrieked and left with it.

Annalie laughed. "Why, you've scared the Captain."

"I despise that beast," Miss Rashten snapped.

"And it despises you."

"You hush if you don't want 'the Captain' to meet a bad end with a potato sack and the reflection pool. Linza, come on. We'll find that girl somewhere."

"I bet Miss Nimira ran off without even saying good-bye," Linza said. Her acting was a bit heavy-handed, but I appreciated her attempt to cover me, and no one seemed to notice.

Annalie waited a moment before she told me to come out. She was pouring out some cream into her saucer for the Captain. "Cruel woman," she said. "That was close."

"And Hollin was going to leave you to Smollings's and Rashten's mercy while he goes abroad?" I asked, appalled.

"Hollin, I'm afraid, is as much at Smollings's mercy as I am. He didn't mean for all this to happen. I'm saddened that he meant to go abroad and leave me here, but truth be told, I've expected it for a long time. Sometimes I've even wished he *would* go. It's almost easier to bear my fate alone than see it reflected in his eyes—see his guilt."

I nodded. "I heard he used dark magic to try to save you."

"Yes," she agreed. "Not unlike the dark magic you must use now to save Erris."

Could I end up like Annalie? Shut up in darkness, talking to the dead?

"Tell me what to do," I said.

22

At the moment, I feared an encounter with Miss Rashten more than any dark magic. Annalie ordered me to get some rest. "You'll need your strength."

While she listened for Miss Rashten's return to her own bedroom, I lay on her bed, but could not sleep. Maybe it was all in my head, but I felt the presence of ghosts. In the darkness, I saw things out the corner of my eye. I felt feather-light touches on my back and heard whispers. By the time Annalie returned, I was more exhausted than before and quite ready for a cup of her coffee.

"I can tell you an incantation to open the gate to the other side," she said. "But your feelings matter more than your words. You must pull the Lady toward you, with all your soul. But be careful. If the gate stays open for too long, the dark spirits will find it. They'll try to enter and possess you. You'll know when they're coming because the room will grow dark and cold."

"What do I do if they try and possess me?"

"I'm not sure I'm the one to ask. I can only tell you that it isn't such a horrid fate, to be possessed. Most of the time the good spirits will keep away the bad, and they are lovely company."

"Oh." I'm sure it was plain on my face that I was horrified at the idea of sharing a similar fate.

She smiled. "The spirits shy away from light. Light a candle to fend them off."

She wished me luck, and I slipped into the hall. The door creaked as I opened it, loud as firing cannons. Miss Rashten's door was closed, but I was sure she must have heard it, even in sleep. I couldn't breathe until I reached the bottom of the stairs, and stopped to be sure I heard nothing behind me.

I fetched a candle and matches from my bedroom, clutching them against my chest beneath my nightgown, my left hand closed around his key, and slipped through the door to Erris's room. I had never been awake at such an hour in my life.

I shut and locked it behind me. I wondered if I should wind Erris for company.

No. If nothing happened, I couldn't bear another good-bye. If the dark spirits came and possessed me, he would be helpless to come to my aid.

I sat in the center of the floor and struck the match. The candle flame rose to life, its golden light casting trembling shadows. The red heels of Erris's shoes glowed. I wondered if he had toes beneath his shoes.

Focus, Nim.

I didn't know how it was supposed to feel to pull with my soul, but my desire to free Erris was surely as strong as any more

experienced sorcerer's summons. I whispered the words Annalie
had taught me:

> O Queen, I have lit you a beacon
> O Queen, I have opened the door
> O Queen, I permit you to enter
> O Queen, I request your aid
>
> Queen of the Longest Night, come to me!

With every word, I clenched my fingers and wished with all my
being, and as I finished, the candle went out.

I reached for the matches. There was no draft, no reason for
the candle to snuff. I held the match to strike, but something
stopped me.

I looked at Erris, and realized there was light in the room that
had not been there before, a light that cast his skin in a faint blue. I
looked at my own hands. They felt suddenly cold, and I clasped
them, trying to rub out the chill. Blue cold radiated from the floors
and walls like winter had come in a moment. I got to my feet, shivering. I picked up the candle, still unlit.

When I looked up, I gasped.

A woman was there. Standing near the wall. She had appeared
without a sound, without a flash.

"I don't have much time," she said. Her voice was firm, even
deep, lacking any mystical air.

She was the warrior woman of the statue in New Sweeling's
square, with a sword at her waist, only full of calm strength and
beauty that was surprisingly benevolent. Tall as a man, old and

ageless at once, with black hair hanging loose, and a faint light radiating from her being. She wore a short cape pinned around her shoulders. A painted bird in flight spread its wings across the breast of her leather bodice.

I couldn't speak, and seeing my fear, she smiled. A kind smile, like the portrait in the palace of Tiansher. I fell to my knees and touched my forehead to the ground, the only way I knew to treat a queen. My heart was pounding.

"I don't have much time," she repeated. I peered forward to see her shoes draw closer. "I can't stay long here. Tell me your request."

"I wish for Erris—this automaton—to live. He is a fairy, trapped in this form. I don't know if there's anything you can do, but Karstor said—and then Annalie said—well, it doesn't matter, just that you do what you can for him, even if it means taking him with you, I suppose—although I hope—" I cut myself off. I hardly knew what I was saying.

She reached down and put her hand atop my head. I rose my face to her, overcome with gratitude that she had come, and that she was kind. Her hand slipped to my chin and drew me up. I nearly stumbled on my nightgown.

"Dear girl," she said. "You need not fear me. It's your love for Erris that brought me here, and with love I come to you."

"Thank you. I don't have words—"

"You don't need words. I understand." She smiled a little. "Only, we must hurry. It won't be an easy spell to break." She began to walk the edge of the room, sprinkling ashen dust she took from a pouch at her waist. "If you'll allow me, I'll see what I might do. I'm going to open the spirit channels, and I must not be disturbed. You can sit down if you like."

The Queen was so lovely, standing over Erris, her eyes

half-lidded in deep concentration. She took more dust from the pouch and sprinkled it upon his head. She murmured, her voice lower than ever, the words strange.

I stood near the door, fascinated by her demeanor and costume, by her leather boots and her skirt with three tiers of fringe, and the pantaloons beneath. The costume would surely look absurd on a woman of Lorinar, but on her it was magnificent. She had capable hands. I imagined she could lead an army, on a white horse, fighting for a righteous cause.

Her voice crept louder. Her hands worked as if reeling in a net above Erris's head. It was hypnotic, its own kind of song and dance. The fringe on her skirt shivered. Her knees moved slightly. Her whole body was involved in the spell.

I heard a faint call, in the direction of my bedroom. "Nimira!" A little louder, "Nimira?"

I gasped, scrambling to my feet. "Hollin. Hollin's looking for me." I went to the door. "He's coming."

"Don't—" She spoke brusquely. "Pay him no mind. I must not be disturbed . . . just—for a moment." She didn't even look my way.

I stayed standing. He was still calling my name, drawing closer. Any moment, he would be at the door.

The Queen's chant took on more urgency.

"Nimira?" He was quite close now.

The doorknob rattled. "Nimira, are you in there? Open the door!"

The Queen glanced to me, and she gasped herself—who knew the Queen of the Dead could gasp? It was not a gentle gasp, but a pained one—like she had been struck. She stepped back from Erris and held her palms out, warding off something unseen.

The blue light around her dimmed. I heard the faintest cruel whisper—where did it come from? From within the room? Inside my own head? It had no direction. And Hollin was still shouting at me.

"They've broken through," the Queen said, speaking as if she were making a great effort to sound calm. "They're coming. You must light your candle. If it goes out, you must light it again. Don't fear them."

"The dark spirits?"

"Yes. Outlaws of my realm." She was dissipating into a haze. "They can't hurt you if you're strong."

"Wait, don't go!" I cried, reaching for her, although I stopped short of trying to actually touch her.

"I must go, Nimira. The longer I leave the channel open, the more of them will come through. Light the candle. You can fight them off. You have all the strength you need. And—take care of him." She touched Erris's shoulder and her eyes were sad.

"Take care of him?" Nothing had changed on his clockwork form. As soon as I looked at him, she slipped from the corners of my eyes like she had never been.

"Wait! Queen! Can't you come back? I—" No answer. The shadows were falling on me, blotting even the moonlight from the window. The whispers grew louder. *Touch her grab her grind her bones drape her swarm her shadows shadows endless . . .*

It was like the lights had turned out on all the world. I could see no more of Erris than a silhouette. I couldn't see the candle. I fumbled on the floor. The wooden boards were cold as slabs of ice and stung my hands. My teeth chattered. I tried to sing to blot out the horrid voices. I hummed scales through my chattering teeth, and still I heard them, like some dreadful poetry. *Dark and endless tomb for maidens unloved untouched forgotten . . .*

I heard a key click, and the door flew open. I heard Hollin's voice, but in the darkness I saw nothing. "Nimira. Nimira!"

"Sir, I—"

"What have you done?"

"I tried—" My hand closed around the matches. I had to light one. I had to light one.

"Nimira—where are you? Come on, get up— God above, this darkness . . . It's happening again—"

"I have to light the candle!"

Hollin barked strange words, and suddenly, a soft light glowed in his hands. No sooner had it appeared than it began to shrink, and he shouted, even louder now— He sounded pained. The light expanded. His arms were glowing, and he grabbed me by the shoulder with warm fingers. The candle dropped from my hand and clattered to the ground.

"Come on!" he cried. "For God's sake, come on!"

We ran. The voices retreated from my head. I ran as fast as I could, but he was still dragging me along, shouting his spells. When I looked back, I saw the shadows melting out from the room into the corridor.

He flung me from him, away from the shadows. "Go back, get into your room. I have to send them away."

"Erris—"

"What?" He shoved me so hard I almost lost my balance. "Never mind, just go. I *won't* lose you, too. *Go,* damn you!"

I streaked down the halls, hugging myself tight. What had I done? Oh, what had I done?

I now understood what Hollin had faced, fighting for Annalie's life. That darkness . . . those horrible voices . . .

Hollin was out of sight now. I stopped to breathe. Behind me I heard him shouting.

I still had the matches in my hand.

I tore into my room and grabbed another of my candles. I forced myself to block out the sound of Hollin's shouting. I must focus. I must light the candle.

I struck the match and touched the wick, just beneath the glass holder.

A steady flame rose. I picked it up and ran. Hollin's arms still glowed, but shadow draped the rest of him. I couldn't see that he'd made any ground. Shadow fingers sunk into the wallpaper and the floors. The husky voices whispered in my head, louder and louder the closer I came. The candle flickered wildly.

"No. No! Get back." I didn't know any spell words, but I could shout. "Get back. Go back to where you came from!"

Hollin kept up his chanting, but I thought his voice strengthened with my arrival. We could win. We would.

The candle flame still danced, threatening extinction. Softly, I began again to sing familiar words I'd heard my mother sing countless times, that I had sung night after night on Granden's stage.

My voice gained strength, easing into a melody it knew so well. My throat filled with music. It pushed back the cold. The candle flame tried to straighten out. I willed it to stand.

There was so much darkness. I imagined the shadows were even in my lungs, straining my breath— No, I must not think of them. I was strong, stronger now than ever. I had come a long way from the girl who had grown up with servants and sashes, the girl who had left home to flee farm work and Father's disgrace.

I stepped farther into the darkness. I must take out its heart. Hollin put his back to mine, walking with me as in a dance. We both understood what must be done.

Drag you down down far away no home no father no mother . . .

My voice faltered as my ears began to listen. *No . . . don't listen.*

Hollin rushed into the silence. "Victory for all the masses; freedom comes for all the classes—!" He took up a tune of Lorinar's independence, a common song for national holidays. I joined in, for I knew the chorus, at least. "Praise to country, man's glory—hail to precious liberty!"

We sang together. I couldn't tell if we were making progress yet. I shut my eyes and shouted the lyrics for all I was worth.

I was afraid to open them when the song ran out.

"I am not afraid!" I suddenly shouted. I realized I was no longer shivering. The cold had lifted from my arms in the course of our song. "I am not afraid! I am not afraid!"

A lower voice joined with mine. Hollin was shouting, too.

When I opened my eyes again, the shadows were slipping away like they had come, melting back into the walls. Hollin and I started to fan out, still shouting like we were driving back stray dogs. We were winning now, and my exhilaration roared in my ears. In the moment, we were triumphant, united. The voices in my head died away with groans and sighs.

Finally, the moonlight shone once more, a gentle light that seeped from the window at the end of the hall, and my candle cast its golden glow.

Hollin and I turned to face each other.

"You're safe," he said. His hand cupped my cheek.

"I—I'm sorry."

He flung his arms around me. Suddenly, this reserved man was all abandon. He pressed me so tight against him that I could hardly find air.

"I was so scared, Nimira. I thought I'd lose you, too. I—I—just, thank God. Thank God. We won. We've done it."

I nodded against his chest, so awash with relief that I had forgotten everything else.

"You were wonderful," Hollin said. "I could never have done it without you. When I faltered, you fought . . . I had to fight for Annalie alone and I lost her, but you—"

"Annalie," I repeated. Her name reminded me just why I had tried such a dangerous spell to begin with.

He released his hold. "Who is Erris?"

"The—the automaton." I had tried everything now. I could tell him.

"The fairy prince?" Hollin furrowed his brow. I thought he'd be angry, but just then he only seemed perplexed. "You know his name? He spoke to you?"

"I would have told you, only I thought you'd send me away. Or send him away. I thought you'd let Smollings destroy him! Anyway, it doesn't matter—the Queen didn't get to unwind the spell and now it's no good, only, only, you mustn't destroy him, *please*. She told me to take care of him."

He released his hold on me and stalked back into the room where Erris should have been sitting erect at his pianoforte. I rushed after him, nearly colliding with his back as he stopped short. I peered around him.

Erris was on the floor, fallen on his side.

I dropped quickly to his side. I brushed back his bangs. His skin was warm and soft. *Oh . . . oh . . . !* I didn't dare hope, yet . . .

I put my fingers to his throat, trying to feel a pulse, but his eyelashes fluttered before I could.

He blinked, and squinted at me. A glorious, wondering smile spread on his lips. "Nim?"

"You're . . . *alive.*"

"How?" His hand lifted to my cheek, the very same place Hollin had just touched. I couldn't believe it. He was real and living, flesh and bone. He looked just like his clockwork form, a young man, attractive and brown-eyed, but he was utterly different. He smelled like pines and autumn. I wanted to press my nose to his coat. His face was full of the motion and detail that only a living thing could have. My eyes traced the dent above his lips, the little pink moist corners of his eyes, the barest stubble on his chin, the heavy lids of his eyes, the full brows . . . I could have looked at him for hours in speechless wonder.

"I—I summoned the Queen of the Longest Night," I said.

He put a hand on the floor and pushed himself into a sitting position before clambering shakily to his feet. "I'm alive. I'm alive." He kept repeating it, like it might cease to be true. "I'm alive." He spread his fingers and turned his hands over.

I realized my own lips reflected his smile. I couldn't seem to *stop* smiling.

I covered my mouth and looked at Hollin.

"What have you done?" he cried. "What shall we do with a fairy prince, brought back from the dead?" He grabbed me and shook me. *"What have you done?"*

Erris stepped between us, pushing Hollin back none too gently. "Calm down. Let Nim go."

Erris was alive. Erris was speaking. Even with Hollin's tension, even though Hollin had shaken me, I couldn't stop wondering at this miracle.

"What are we to do with him?" Hollin said again. "What will Smollings say to this? How could we even explain?" His fingers spread and searched like he wished to hold on to something that made sense.

"There's no need to shout." Erris was starting to sound a little angry himself. "I don't want to cause trouble. I'm going to see Karstor."

"Karstor!" Hollin cried. "I'll be damned if you're off to see him! Smollings would ... My God, I don't even know what he'd do."

"You don't get to decide anymore," Erris said. "I'm alive." He stopped and touched his hand to his temple in sudden disbelief. He reached for my hand. "Nim, I can't believe you really did it."

"And you feel fine? You're really alive?"

He put his hand over his heart. "Yes. I think so." The briefest concern knit his brows. Hollin and I both noticed.

"How could this even have happened?" Hollin said. "I doubt even the Lady could make flesh and blood from nothing."

"I must be alive," Erris said. He looked down at his chest, inhaling and exhaling to watch it rise and fall. "Or else ... well, what's all this?"

"I don't know, but the Sorcerer's Council will have to see about it," Hollin said. "The council has to approve bringing someone back from the dead. I think other forces must be at work."

"Stop it, Hollin. You're scaring him."

"I should be scaring you, Nimira. You're the one who did this, and the council will decide your fate, too. The council headed by

Smollings." He held his hands out, almost pleadingly, and said once more, softer now, "What have you done?"

"There must be something we can do," I said. I was beginning to grow frightened indeed. Smollings would probably be happy to lock me away and use Erris for his own purposes. I had never thought what to do afterward, if I actually brought Erris to life. I supposed I thought he would protect me, but he was a fairy on human turf, and his own people would have considered him dead for some thirty years.

"I want to see Karstor and I want Nim to come with me," Erris said.

"'Nim' is my fiancée."

I inhaled sharply, ready to protest, when Erris spoke again.

"You don't treat her like the woman you love."

"Because she's been sneaking around in the middle of the night casting dark magic! I'm hardly going to gather her into a loving embrace, considering the circumstances!" Hollin's hands slowly curled into fists, relaxed again, curled again—Erris tapped his palm to his hip like he was checking for a weapon.

"Wait—please, let's be reasonable," I said, only this was no ordinary case of two suitors dueling for a woman's hand. I had hoped Erris might live again, but seeing him before me as a real man, I hardly knew what to do or think or say . . .

Erris suddenly clutched his chest.

I grabbed his arm. "What's wrong?"

"I—" He staggered. "I'm winding down . . . !"

His knees gave out from under him, and all at once he was crumpled on the ground again, his face mashed into the hard floor, a pose no conscious person would have borne. I cried out and dropped to his side again, reaching for his wrist, trying to find the beat of life. Hollin got down with me. "Get back," he said, pushing aside Erris's coat. His shirt still had an open back for his clockwork mechanism, and there in the center of his back, interrupting the line of his spine, was a small metal plate, with a keyhole in it.

23

"So that's how she brought him to life," Hollin murmured. "He's still an automaton, only she animated the clockwork body in absence of a corpse..."

I didn't even hear Hollin at first. I stared at that dreadful keyhole, unable to believe this impossible reality. The shock seared through every nerve in my body, paralyzing me. Could it be true? Had I really brought Erris into such an unnatural life, at the mercy of a silver key?

I had left the key on the floor and now I reached for it, but Hollin saw me. He snatched it first, holding it against his chest.

"Wind him!" I said, as if he would follow my command.

"No one is winding him." Hollin tapped his palm with the key. I don't think he really knew what to do.

"But there are so many questions to ask him—"

"Nimira, I am flabbergasted by your lack of concern with the situation as a whole. Do you know what you did? How close you came to death, or worse? If I hadn't come along—"

"Everything was fine *until* you came along! The Queen was very kind. She—"

"*Hush!*"

I realized how exhausted I was. I didn't have energy for this kind of fight. Why couldn't he just understand? Poor Erris had finally found life, only to collapse on the floor, still clockwork, after all. The ramifications were more than I wanted to consider.

"We're supposed to be departing on the voyage of a lifetime," Hollin said. "Instead, you've saddled us with this. If we leave now, I could still save you from Smollings, but we'd have to do something with *him*."

"Hollin, you know I can't leave with you now."

"And you know you can't save him!" Hollin cried. "Listen carefully, Nimira. Smollings is head of the council and his allies have the council majority. If you stay here, he will have the automaton and he can put you in prison if he wishes. You've placed us all in a very bad position."

I stared at the floor. I had thought bringing Erris to life would put everything right. Now this seemed an utterly foolish hope. I had to get the key from Hollin somehow, but I couldn't just ask for it. Could I ask Annalie for help again? Miss Rashten would surely be on alert now.

I didn't really know what to do anymore.

"Well, Nimira." Hollin spoke softly. "Have you nothing to say?"

"You dare to accuse me of putting us in a bad situation?" I asked, my anger burning all the brighter for my lack of solutions. "You told me you used dark magic to try and save Annalie. You told me Smollings is using it to blackmail you. But you didn't tell me that she's still alive!"

He took a step closer to me, and I took a step back. "Who told you?" he asked.

"No one. I found her."

"Have you seen her?"

"Of course I've seen her. She ran into my room that night, begging for help, if you recall!"

Anguish swept his face. "She didn't know what she was saying. And she's not the same anymore. She hears voices, Nimira. She speaks to spirits; they *got* to her. She has spells where I wonder if she even knows me."

"I've just been to see her," I said, hoping I wouldn't make more trouble for Annalie by mentioning her involvement, but it didn't seem like things could get worse anyway. "She was quite kind to me. She didn't seem like the madwoman you described. She deserves better treatment than being left alone while you run off with me."

"Why didn't you say something before?"

"I figured you'd send me away. And I needed to save Erris."

He scowled. "I don't know what you would have me do."

"You could tell the truth about her. You could, at least, do that much."

He looked at Erris's limp form, and then he met my eyes for the first time since we had entered the room. "I am ... truly sorry I brought you into this. But it's bigger than we have the power to change. You've acted without thinking of the consequences."

"You're one to speak to me of acting without thinking of consequences!" I said.

Hollin looked away, tucking Erris's key inside his pocket. "Go back to bed."

24

Sometimes, before you make any plans or resolutions, before you declare your heroic intent to persevere, you just have to cry.

And cry I did.

I may have slept; it was hard to be sure. When morning crept through the crack in my curtains, I was crying again, soft sobs that came almost unconsciously. My head was buried in my arms at the little table where I ate breakfast. One of my braids had come undone.

Someone rapped on my door.

I didn't lift my head. "Go away." I sounded hoarse.

"Nonsense." It was Miss Rashten, not the *very* last person I wanted to see, but certainly on the list. "I have your breakfast."

"I don't want breakfast."

The doorknob rattled. I had locked it. I heard her keys jingle. With a whispered curse, I got to my feet and flung the door open.

She smiled a little at my vexed expression. "Well, well," she said, shoving past me into the room. "You thought you were quite crafty, didn't you? Sneaking around behind my back, in cahoots with the Mistress. I hope you enjoyed your little escapade." She dumped the breakfast tray on my table and arched a brow at me.

"I don't want to talk," I said, reaching for my chair.

She kicked the chair from me with her foot and seized my nightgown by the ruffles decorating the front. "Enjoy your defiance while you can, girl. When Master Smollings gets hold of you, you'll talk when he wants you to—and only then."

"How dare you touch me," I snapped, wrenching from her grasp.

"I might ask you, miss, how *you* dare. To snoop upstairs where Hollin told you not to go, to summon the Lady. From the moment you arrived, you've been trouble."

We stared each other down. Her blue eyes drooped at the corners and bagged underneath; old eyes, but they had not softened with their years. Some old women you can never imagine young, but you could picture Miss Rashten in an awkward sort of youth. I guessed she had not been happy, probably the type who couldn't flirt and never seemed to dress right, who came into her power when she got past the time when such things mattered.

"I owe Mr. Smollings my life," she said, still staring at me. "If you think fairies and spirits are such wonderful creatures, try living near the gate. A group of fairies would have killed me if he hadn't come to my aid, back in his days as chief of the border patrol. So you'll understand why I have very little tolerance for your antics."

A sudden shout turned both our heads to the door. Hollin. Something crashed.

Miss Rashten rushed to the hall, and I came just behind her, pulling my other braid loose, my bare feet sticking to the wood floors, and my robe and nightgown—well, Hollin had already seen me in a nightgown before.

Erris was darting around the chairs in the great hall, gripping a cushion in one hand, while Hollin put up a chase, holding his sorcerer's staff at a threatening angle. A vase had shattered on the floor, and Linza stood back with a broom, looking far too terrified to clean anything.

Erris halted, holding the cushion like a shield. They looked like boys playing a game of chase, except for the serious expressions.

"Stay back, Nimira," Hollin said. "He's gone wild. Tore the door handle right off."

"You're the one who stormed out and locked me up!" Erris shouted.

"For your own *good*."

"That had nothing to do with my own good! You just didn't care for the questions I was asking!" Erris threw the pillow down onto the nearest chair. "Why don't we have it all out, right here in the hall, with Nimira? This concerns her, too." Erris waved a hand to me. He still had on his fairy clothes, a festive antique costume more fit for a palace than Vestenveld's somber interiors.

"There is nothing to have out with Nimira," Hollin said. "She isn't part of this decision. Neither are you, for that matter. The Sorcerer's Council will decide what to do with you."

Erris cupped his hands in front of him. It seemed to be a fairy gesture of supplication. "Please. All I want is to go home."

Hollin shook his head. "I can't let you go. You're the heir."

"No," Erris said. "You must understand, I don't wish for the throne. I'm sure whichever brother or sister is ruling is doing a fine job. I just want my old life back. Or what I can find of it now. My piano, and my . . . well, my hound will be very much dead."

I didn't want Hollin to tell him, but I knew he would, and I knew Erris must know.

"Your brothers and sisters are gone," Hollin said. "They were all killed in the war."

"Not . . . all of them? I knew about Peri and Rennin and . . . Aria." His face seemed to age five years in an instant. "There were ten of us. They can't all be dead." He brought his hands tight against his chest, and I briefly feared he would rend his clothes, but he kept calm. "Who is king now?"

"Graweldin," Hollin said. "Luka Graweldin."

"Luka?" Erris cried. "My cousin? The one who always ran a victory lap around the lawn when he beat me at toss-rings?"

Erris stared at Hollin like he truly wanted an answer. Hollin finally said, "I . . . presume."

Erris's face was alarmingly blank. I should have merely been happy he was alive, but what world had I granted him? His family was dead. He lived only as a prisoner to whoever held the silver key. What balm could I offer to a wound so gaping as the loss of one's family? Perhaps death would have been more merciful. I still couldn't bear the thought, but was I only being selfish?

Hollin looked at me. I did not expect this moment, this sympathy that suddenly flashed across his eyes. We had both tried to save someone with the most desperate means. And in our way, we had both failed.

I saw something wake in Hollin's eyes then as he looked at me and then to Erris again. Something that went beyond sympathy and verged upon strength.

Hollin took a step toward Erris.

Erris's jaw was clenched with the effort of keeping his composure.

"I am sorry for your loss," Hollin said stiffly. He opened his hand. The key rested in his palm. "Take it."

Erris hesitated. He was obviously as startled as I was by the sudden offer.

"Take it and go!" Hollin shouted. "Both of you, go."

Erris snatched the key and stepped back again. He glanced at me.

"Where can we go?" I said. "To—to Karstor's?" I didn't know if we could escape without Hollin's help . . . but with it?

"Where does he live?" Erris asked.

I shook my head.

"I can tell you where he lives," Hollin said. "I could even lend you a carriage. But Miss Rashten knows who you are and what you are, which means Smollings will know before long. I wouldn't be surprised if you cross him on your way to find Karstor. Supposing you make it to Karstor's without getting caught, supposing he's even home, he could try and get you to the border, but it's three days away, and who will help you once you're across? I don't suppose the fairy king will be too happy to see the lost heir. And what will the council do to Karstor once they learn he's smuggled you out? You are putting him in certain peril."

"So you're saying it's hopeless?" Erris said.

"I'm just stating facts," Hollin said. "I'll leave the choice to you. I'm . . . tired. I don't care anymore." He stalked from the room.

Miss Rashten had watched the whole thing from the doorway. I had no doubt she was already forming her own plans about what to do if we tried to flee.

Erris turned the key over. He gripped it in his fist. "Nim."

For the first time, we had our chance to really talk. I approached slowly, until I stood before him, and our eyes met.

He reached for my hand—his skin so alive—and pressed the key into my limp fingers. He folded them around it, his hands closed on my own.

"I'm so sorry," I said.

He shook his head. "Sorry? No. Don't be sorry."

"But . . . I didn't mean for it to happen like this."

"Don't think for a moment this is your fault. I haven't had an ordinary life in a long time. You did what you could, and look—now we can talk. At last." He smiled, and his eyes roamed a little lower.

I furrowed my eyebrows. "Are you looking at my bosom, sir?"

The eyes snapped back up. "At such a serious moment? What do you take me for?"

"A rogue, I believe." I tried not to smile.

He held out his elbow. "Well, fair lady. Let's walk in the garden. It will help me to think."

"I'm still wearing my nightgown."

With a nervous glance to Miss Rashten, Linza broke from her side. "I'll get you dressed right quick, Miss Nimira."

Miss Rashten lifted her head like she might call out to stop us, but instead she snatched up her dustpan and headed for the door.

Linza led me back to my room, where she brought forth one of my most fetching outfits, a white day dress with lace inserts on the bodice and finely worked white embroidery detail on the skirt.

"Oh, I'm not sure about that one," I said. "I'm not really in a white dress mood, Linza. How about the old plaid?"

"The old plaid!" Linza cried. "Miss *Nimira*." She gave me an exasperated face and raised her eyebrows. "It's not my place to question you, but I will say that while I'm not sure exactly what happened with the automaton, he is a *very* handsome man now, and *very* finely dressed."

"Oh, all right, all right." I motioned for the white dress.

25

"Oh, Nim," he said, when I emerged in the dress. Such a face he made, like he was so grateful just to see me, just to take my hand, that he didn't know whether to laugh or cry. I was shivering all over from the sheer emotion of it, and I couldn't seem to stop. We slipped out the back door together and walked down the steps to the garden.

I still couldn't believe Erris was real. I had to wrap my fingers around my skirt to keep from touching him. I worried that he might be torn from me, as quickly as he'd come. Every moment felt so precious that I wondered if I could enjoy a single one.

I'd almost forgotten that he hadn't seen trees and plants in some thirty years. His gaze followed the butterflies, and every leaf and flower received a glancing touch from his hand. Finally, he threw his hands up to the sky, worshipping the golden sun.

"This is amazing. The world is amazing. Look—look at that squirrel!"

"That's a squirrel, indeed." I tried to smile. A shawl of sorrow rested heavy on my shoulders, but I didn't want to ruin his moment of joy when we both knew there was no guarantee of more.

"Lord, Nim, a squirrel! I haven't seen one in—well, too long. I won't dwell on that. And look at the sky! It's so blue! It's devastating, how blue that sky is. I could see only a little of it out my window, out of the corner of my eye, but there it is, so broad . . ." He ran his hand across the sky, like he could touch the very clouds.

The wind teased my hair, which still hung loose. Erris caught a strand and tucked it behind my ear. He placed his hands just below my shoulders, his grip heavy. His eyes were a deep brown.

"This is strange, isn't it," he said. "It's strange to be here, and you don't know what to do with me. I don't know what to do with me."

"Should we . . . try and go to Karstor's?"

"I don't know if I even want to go home anymore. I wanted to see my family, what was left of them. If they're gone— If Luka is king . . ." He sighed. "I suppose this means Garvin hoped to restore me to life so he could put me on the throne instead."

"Yes. Something like that."

"He didn't tell me," Erris said. "He should have told me my family was dead. I could have told him to save himself the trouble. I'm not fit to be a *king*." He started walking faster. "Especially not now that I'm some sort of walking, breathing . . . clockwork!"

"Erris!" He was running now, outpacing me. I tried to catch up, but my slippers weren't made for chasing, and the pretty Verrougian corset was even more unforgiving to my heaving ribs than the one I'd worn running from Granden. He went through the bower, out of my sight.

When I caught up, he had an arm around the willow tree that dangled its green tears in the pond. Lily pads floated on the surface, and in the center, a fat duck paddled along in perfect contentment, but Erris didn't see it. His eyes were shut against the world.

"I can't feel the trees anymore," he said, and he sounded so heartbroken, like he'd lost another sister or brother.

"I'm so sorry," I said. "Erris, I'm so sorry! I thought I was helping you, but I've made everything awful. I thought everything would fall into place if you were only alive again. I thought we could stop Smollings. I must have seen too many stage shows. It was all some romantic idea, and now you're stuck, and I wish I knew what to do, but I don't."

"Nim, no. No." He put a hand to my back. "You gave me a gift. When your life is frozen—all you want is this. Just to move, and see the sky, simple things like that. You've given me that." He watched a flock of birds scatter from a tree. "If Smollings destroys me, at least I could look him in the eye first."

"Erris . . ."

"I didn't mean to sound ungrateful," he said. "You risked a lot for me. The problems are much bigger than you, and they'd be worse if you weren't here. And I can speak to you. I wanted that more than I can say." He smiled faintly. "I'm not going to lie. I thought about you a lot. I mean, of course, whenever I was wound, you were there. But in the between-times, I lived in a sort of dream . . . and you were there, too."

I thought about how I had kissed his lips. And now he was a real man . . .

"I thought about you, too," I said.

Erris reached for my hand. "Well, if this is my chance to talk to you, I'd better try not to squander it."

We crossed around the side of the house, but we strayed off the path, trudging through a sloping field of overgrown grass. I gathered up my dress so I wouldn't dirty the lace hem. Crickets danced out of our path. Erris picked a white spray of flowers and twirled the stem between his fingers. Just then, the world was all beauty and sunshine, with the breeze teasing our hair. It didn't seem like anything bad could happen.

I searched for some topic of discussion so we would not merely brood in silence.

"Now that you can speak, can you tell me any more about how you became an automaton?"

He frowned. "I'm not sure I know much more myself, but at least I can give you a little more background of what led to it. The humans attacked us at a time when our family was already vulnerable. My father was getting very old, and while my eldest brother should have been the obvious choice for succession, he wasn't very well liked."

"Do you think that cousin of yours had something to do with it, too? Not just the humans?"

"I think so. He was a distant cousin, and that branch of the family had never gotten along well with my father's people. For a number of reasons." Erris seemed to be momentarily lost in memories of what must have been a very complicated family. He continued, "I think Luka and his family may have made a deal with human sorcerers, like Smollings—or maybe his father, or Hollin's father." He rolled his eyes a little. "I do wish I'd paid more attention to the situation then."

"What were you doing?"

"Oh, I was having fun!" He laughed. "Well, wars have a way of sneaking up on you. You don't want to believe your world is changing, and at first it's all very stirring to see parades and soldiers assembling all that. It doesn't hit you until someone you love dies. . . ."

"You didn't fight?"

"In my country, you don't fight until you're twenty. Unless, of course, times are very dire. The sorcerers got me before it came to such a point."

"Where did they catch you?"

He groaned a bit. "You're going to think I'm such a fool, Nim! We'd had reports of humans nearby and my mother told me not to leave the palace, but I thought she was overreacting, so I snuck out in a disguise to visit some friends in town. It obviously wasn't a very good disguise. And she obviously wasn't overreacting."

"Well, you're right. You should have listened to your mother. But I imagine you learned your lesson."

"I certainly did . . ." His expression took a serious turn. "At first they just held me in a room and questioned me, and I thought it might be all right, but then . . . they did whatever they did." He shook his head. "It all gets hazy after that."

"Does it feel like all those years have passed?"

This question sobered him more. "I don't think you were even born when I was last walking around . . . How strange. It does feel like time has passed, but not the way it should. My family, my home, they all seem far away, but until Garvin found me there's been nothing to fill the space but dreams and shadows." He looked at his palms, flexing his wrists, as if affirming that he could truly move. "And what now? I've been given this extraordinary second chance, and I haven't any idea what to do with it."

I pressed my palms to his larger ones, conscious of every point where our skin touched, of the soft warmth of him, of the beauty of this living man walking close to me, and what we had shared. "We've come this far. There must be something we could do."

He laced his fingers with mine, but his smile was faint. "Even if I could escape, I told you I'm not the man to reclaim the family throne."

"Maybe running away isn't the right answer. Maybe we need to do something about Smollings. If there was some way just to stop him. Annalie told me Garvin's spirit visits her sometimes. She said Smollings killed Garvin." I chewed my lower lip. The answers felt so close . . . yet I couldn't fit the puzzle pieces together.

"I knew he did!" Erris cried. "I knew it. That's exactly it, Nim. We need to prove what he did. It's the only way to get justice for Garvin—and maybe undo my enchantment, too."

"I would love to prove it. But how? Would anyone listen to Annalie? No one even knows she's alive!"

"Can't she channel his spirit? Maybe a séance?"

"Is a séance considered legitimate evidence?"

Erris didn't answer. The sound of footsteps crashing through the plants, just around the corner of the wall, halted our conversation. Linza dashed up to us, strands of fair hair floating around her head like a disheveled halo under the sunshine, a broom in her hand.

"Smollings!" she panted. "He's here!"

26

"Already?" My heart was suddenly racing, and I wanted to grab Erris's hand and bolt, but where to? The nearest copse of trees wouldn't hide us. Could we make it to the forest?

"They said he came galloping up, alone on horseback, like he hadn't slept all night. Miss Rashten must have got a message through to him somehow."

Erris put an arm around me. It would have felt more reassuring if it wasn't for the nervous clench of his fingers. "If we run I think we'll only give him the satisfaction of chasing us."

"But what shall we say to him?"

"I'd help you fight him," Linza offered, and I felt sheepish that she currently seemed to be the bravest among us. "I'd hit him with my broom. Miss Rashten already has it out for me anyway."

"That's all right," I said quickly, as I heard approaching male voices. "Go back to the house." I didn't want to implicate Linza in this mess any more than she already was.

I heard Hollin say something in a sharp tone, and Smollings's equally sharp reply, but I couldn't make out the words.

The men quieted down as they came around the wall. Sweat had soaked through Smollings's jacket, and his face was haggard with exhaustion, but he carried himself with the greatest dignity. He held his sorcerer's staff, the one I had seen him touch Annalie with to make her cry out in pain.

"So it's true," Smollings said. "The lost fairy prince, in the flesh. So to speak."

Erris lowered his eyelids, giving Smollings an imperious look.

Smollings turned to me. "Well, Nimira. You are a very fortunate girl, to have managed this, without being consumed by the spirits of the netherworld."

"Of course I wasn't consumed," I said, as if fighting them off hadn't been one of the most harrowing experiences of my life, as if I didn't care if he threw me in prison.

"Bravado is most unbecoming in a woman," Smollings said. "So. A living automaton. I hardly believed it when the message came, but now I see." He looked at Hollin. "Is he still wound by a key?"

Hollin said nothing.

"Miss Rashten told me you still had to wind him. Where is the key?" He stepped toward Erris. "Turn around. I want to see this botched magic."

Erris held up his hands, like he'd push Smollings if he dared touch him. "Why would you need to see?" he snapped.

Smollings smiled at Hollin. "And he's temperamental, I see. Has he given you any trouble?"

Hollin looked at Erris, the air nearly crackling between them, and then said no.

"Oh, very good. I'm glad you're agreeable, Prince. If you

continue to be agreeable, we might come to some sort of arrangement."

Erris stood perfectly still except for his hands, which slowly curled into fists.

"I'm taking you both back to New Sweeling," Smollings said, motioning me forward, which I naturally ignored. "Hollin, give me his key."

"I'll give you his key if you don't take Nimira," Hollin said.

"Nimira? For god's sake, Hollin, don't tell me you're still swooning over a damned trouser girl! Open your eyes. Look what she's done."

"It's my fault," Hollin said, giving me a brief silencing glance. "I brought her here. She acted out of compassion. She doesn't know what she's doing."

Was he trying to protect me? But . . . it would be no good to save me and not Erris.

Smollings furrowed skeptical brows. "Parry, can I talk to you a moment?" He gave Hollin's shoulder a rough pat, urging him back to the garden.

"This is horrid," Erris whispered as they moved just out of sight.

"What can we do?"

Erris took my hands and held them.

"Nim, I think our only chance is to convince Hollin and Annalie to speak out against Smollings. Even if they can't prove he murdered Garvin, they could spur an investigation. If Smollings takes both of us, there's no chance. You need to stay with Hollin."

He was right, and we both knew it, but I didn't want to let him go. Smollings would keep Erris alive for now, most likely, but I didn't trust him.

"I know," Erris said. "I don't want him to ... to wind me. I don't want to give in, but I don't know what else to do."

I clutched my hands to my elbows. I wished I was a sorceress myself, someone who could only laugh at Smollings. I wanted to see his jaw drop. I wanted to see him humiliated. I wished Smollings were the clockwork man who had to be wound; then we'd see how he liked it.

I saw the weary decades in Erris's eyes. "I don't even know how long I'll live," he said. "Is this really life? I'm not really alive, Nim. What if this body breaks down?" His voice had a catch in it. He looked at me and slid his hand up my cheek. "You have to be here, to try and put things right."

His touch prompted my skin to tingle and my lips to tremble.

"Don't look at me like that," he whispered. "I can't stand it. I'm only being honest."

"You can't die." I pressed my hand atop his, holding it fast to my skin. "Don't say that. She brought you to *life*."

Now I started to cry, real sliding tears, although I was ashamed. Erris had enough to worry about without needing to console me. He tried to put his arms around me, and I turned away. "No. I'm not crying like one of those girls—who only wants to be *held*."

"You *do* want to be held." His arms went around me from behind. I felt his strength. "And how I've wanted to hold you, Nim. I *do* like Nim. And I don't just mean the name."

I stopped pushing. I let out my breath. Some resistance inside me broke, letting in a rush of something I'd never allowed before. I had never been so weak; yet I had never been so strong.

I turned in his arms, laying my head against his shoulder. He smelled sweet as summer grass. Our bodies drew closer. He kissed my cheek, gently, like my skin was sacred. My breath came faster, excitement and panic coursing through my veins until I felt dizzy.

"I love you, Nimira." He spoke softly in my ear. "Whatever happens now, I have spoken those words with my own voice, and held you with my own arms."

I hadn't known a person could hold so much joy and so much grief at once. I was speechless with it. I didn't want to ever leave that embrace, and it seemed so cruel, so very cruel, that the force of my feelings couldn't keep me there.

We heard two sets of footsteps returning.

By the time Hollin and Smollings rounded the corner again, Erris and I were standing apart and gravely silent. I had my fingers buried in my pocket, clutched around Erris's key.

Smollings held the other key, the twin to mine. "Here is what will happen," he said. "The fairy will come with me. Nimira, you may stay with Parry. He has pleaded your case to me, but you keep your mouth shut or all bets are off."

I wondered what Hollin had said to convince Smollings to leave me alone. Although I supposed all hope was not lost, it still felt awfully close. I pressed my lips together fast and didn't look at anybody. In fact, no one moved at all.

"Well, then," Smollings said after a moment. "Come on."

Of course I wouldn't put up a fuss. I knew how futile it would be. Yet, how could I stand by and let Smollings take him? Erris would suffer and it was all my fault.

"Please! Please don't take him!" I cried, briefly knowing only that I couldn't bear to see Erris torn from me.

"Nimira, if I were you, I'd hold my tongue," Smollings said. "In fact, I'd kiss Hollin Parry's feet for defending you. I'm sure he'd enjoy it."

I flushed with a shame I should not have felt. I knew I should be grateful that Hollin defended me, but I almost wished he hadn't.

"Where are you taking me?" Erris asked. "You've come alone. Where are the police?"

"This situation requires a sorcerer of high caliber," Smollings said. "Don't worry. I'll ensure that justice is served. I used to be chief of the border patrol, after all."

"This situation?" Erris echoed. "I'm not a 'situation.'"

"You're a fairy and that is enough of a situation," Smollings said. "Your very existence is dangerous. You may think me cruel, but I must act for the good of the country. If you want to live, Prince, you have to accept that your life is not your own. It belongs to the council, and they shall decide your fate."

Smollings held up the key like a dagger with which he would shortly stab Erris in the back. "Say good-bye," he said, looking at us.

"I don't like good-byes," Erris said. He took my hand and kissed it. "I'll see you soon, Nim."

It seemed a long time since I had been the composed Nimira who never cried. I could only nod now.

"All right," Smollings said, and he turned to the house. Erris followed, giving me one last brave smile.

∼ 27 ∼

My attempt to sit alone in my bedroom, weeping quietly into a pillow for a while, was interrupted by Linza's gentle rap on my door.

"Miss Nimira?"

"I'd rather be alone now, Linza. Thank you."

"You haven't eaten all day."

"I know. I'm not hungry."

I heard her body shift against the door. "I'm so sorry about what happened."

I wiped my eyes and finally opened the door. "Oh, Linza... that's all right." I certainly didn't want Linza to think she'd done anything wrong, when the rest of us were already brooding on our mistakes.

"I'm sorry to interrupt, but I came for a reason. Master Parry would like to see you in the tower."

"Why?"

"He didn't say. I'm sorry."

I smiled. "You don't have to keep telling me you're sorry."

In the tower room, Hollin stood by his chair, awaiting me, just as he had on my first day at Vestenveld. I accepted my chair grudgingly. I knew I lacked the energy this conversation would require.

We sat, filling our plates with food I suspected neither of us had any intention of eating.

He buttered a roll. Surely no roll was ever so buttered as that roll was. I wondered if he would ever speak.

"Why did you save me?" I finally asked.

"If Smollings had taken you, he'd probably have put you in prison, and you would likely die there. You understand that, don't you?"

"Mmm." I didn't like this, as if I owed him something now, and yet I was frightened of prison. I'd heard enough tales. As if the poor food and stale air didn't weaken prisoners enough, typhoid and cholera ran rampant. I could hardly think of a more horrifying way to die than the lonely filth of prison.

"What did you say that convinced him to let me stay?"

"I said I would tell the world about his involvement in covering up Annalie. I told him you had just gotten swept into this, that you were inconsequential, and that Miss Rashten would surely keep a close eye on you from now on."

"And what if I wanted to leave this house, knowing all your secrets?"

He shook his head. "I imagine she would stop you."

"So I'm as much a prisoner here as Annalie." I pushed my plate back, disgusted by even the pretense of dinner. "What do you intend to do with me?"

"Nimira, I must be blunt."

"Be blunt, then."

"You will not deny your affections for the fairy now, I'm sure."

"No. I'm sure you must know precisely all my thoughts and feelings." My tongue turned out more vinegar than I intended. "But it no longer matters, does it? He is gone."

Gone. A horrid word, in any language.

He made a faint gasp or sigh, like some small wound had pained him. "Nimira, you must—you must realize how impossible it would have been. You could never have a future with him."

I knew it, perhaps, but I didn't believe it.

"I spoke with him," Hollin continued. "He told me he doesn't want to assume the throne. But it doesn't matter what he wants. He is the lost heir that many of his people have been hoping for. And once the fairies know he's been found, it will have a dramatic impact on their government, not to mention our own relations with the fairy race. Whatever happy ending the two of you may have wished for, you must have known it was impossible."

"Maybe he can't escape being the heir, but surely he can escape Smollings, at least? Maybe Erris is the one to bring peace, the one who can prevent the war you keep implying will happen."

Hollin carefully dusted his food with salt, grimacing all the while. "You'll have a good life here," he said, without much conviction.

"Do you really want to sit back while Lorinar and the fairies go to war?" I asked. "Countless people will die!"

"Well, what do you want me to do? I don't see any way to halt the course we're on. Smollings has Erris and the council will use him to their best advantage."

"Which means he'll take care of Erris the way he took care of Garvin."

Hollin got very still, but his eyes flashed danger. Had I pushed him too far, this man who had already risked a great deal for my sake? If only I could show him he must go further, however painful. He must tell the truth, to me and to the world.

"Well. You've spoken to Annalie, I see." He cut off my response. "Yes. She told me, too. I know what Smollings did. But it's still no use trying to fight him. He's too powerful."

"I would rather fight them than run."

"He'd win, Nimira. He's got the council in his control. He'd ruin us."

"I think he's already ruined you."

"I know he has!" Hollin shouted, his voice ragged. He pounded the table, then buried his head in his hands.

"Hollin, wait," I said. "There is strength in you. I know it. I haven't always been strong either. I ran away from home, and ever since then I've been more lost than ever. You saved me when you took me away from that stage. I would return the favor, if I could."

"But ... you know what I've done. How on earth can I stand against Smollings?"

"But you also know what he's done, don't you?" I met his eyes square. "You know he doesn't want the world to know about how he's using Annalie to access dark spirits. If you confess, you'll prove his part in this, too. He'll suffer more than you will. What do you have to lose at this point?"

For a moment, his expression turned inward. I knew he did still have much to lose. His home, his reputation. But he had already lost everything that truly mattered. If only he understood that.

He did understand. I could see the moment his resolve sharpened, the way his eyes took on the sudden light of purpose. His head lifted. "Very well, Nimira," he said. "We're paying a visit to my wife."

⚬⚬⚬

Curtains still shrouded many of the third-floor windows, but some light trickled through. Hollin led me right to the locked door across from Annalie's old room and took out keys. I had last traced these footsteps in the darkness. He opened the door, bringing us into the small, dim room with windows draped in thick curtains that preceded Annalie's room, and knocked on her door.

I heard Annalie call, with a hint of apprehension, "Yes?"

"Let me in, Anni."

She opened the door right away, a few orbs fluttering behind her. When she saw me, her lips pursed anxiously. "What is going on?"

Hollin motioned for me to go ahead, and when we'd both crossed the threshold, he shut the door. He gave Annalie a long look, full of emotions more deep and numerous than I could read.

She pushed back her hood, which had covered her hair. "What is it?"

Hollin bowed his head a little at her, like a lady he'd passed on the street. "Are you—well?" he asked.

"Well enough," Annalie said. "Please, tell me. Hollin—please. Something has happened." She put her fingers to his shoulder, so delicately that he might have been a soap bubble she feared to break.

"Smollings was here. He took . . . the automaton."

"Erris?" Annalie looked at me. "I heard the spell worked. You brought him back to life?"

"In a way," I said. "He's alive, he moves, but he's still clockwork inside somehow. And now Smollings has him."

"Oh, no," Annalie said, placing her hands over her heart. She looked up at the orbs, as if looking for Garvin among them. Of course, they all looked the same to my eyes. "Yes, yes," she whispered. She didn't seem to be speaking to us. "I know . . ."

"Is Garvin here?" Hollin asked, looking alarmed.

"Not now."

"Could you . . ." Hollin tugged nervously on his necktie. "I'm not sure how it works. Would you be able to summon him on command?"

Annalie clasped her hands, a glimmer in her eyes. "Why?"

"Because . . . I—I have a plan. Or rather, Nimira does. But only if . . . you're willing. I'll need you."

"Most willing," she said, and the orbs danced around her head, as if they, too, were hopeful.

28

Annalie now motioned for me to stand at her side. She squeezed my hand. "What is your plan?"

"It won't be easy," he said. "Smollings has the—Erris. He'll be showing him to the council, to try and prove Garvin had secret plans with the fairies—plans that would lead us into war if Erris were restored to the throne. Smollings has already stirred up a lot of anti-fairy sentiment."

"I thought you agreed with Smollings," Annalie said. One of the orbs hovered near her shoulder, and she brushed it away. "He does," she whispered to it.

Hollin frowned. He seemed very uncomfortable in the presence of Annalie and her orbs, but particularly when she spoke to them.

"Smollings has gone too far," Hollin said. "I still think the fairies are dangerous and no friends of ours, but . . . I am growing increasingly unsettled by Smollings. What he's done to us . . . to you . . . I'm beginning to realize just how dangerous he is—not just for us, but for the country." His pale cheeks flushed, and he shifted his stance. "I don't like Karstor, but he's . . . he's not a *cruel* man."

"There is no question about our plan, then," Annalie said. "We must go to the council."

"And you can . . . summon Garvin?"

"I believe so. I'm sure he'll want to come, when I tell him. But summoning any spirit does take a little time."

Hollin nodded, looking nervous. "Very well, then." His eyes flicked to the door. "The only trouble is Miss Rashten. I know she has powers, but I'm not sure how much. She won't let us leave without a fight. I'm sure of that. And if we do make it out, she'll tell Smollings immediately."

"If you stand with me, then I know we can overcome her," Annalie said, and with her words, she seemed to grow old and ageless at once, like the Queen of the Longest Night. "Ever since the lost souls began visiting me, they tell me things . . . and other things, they didn't have to tell me. I simply *know,* somehow. I'm somewhere between their world and yours now. They'll work for me."

"Anni—I don't care what they've told you. Look what they've done to you."

"You don't understand them as I do. They don't *mean* to hurt people, exactly. Only, when the barriers open, they're like starving men. They can only think of food. They try to possess people because it's their one way to get the only thing they want. They can't die properly without closure, but they can't have closure without life."

"They whisper terrible things," Hollin said. "For beings who supposedly don't mean to hurt us."

"Well . . ." She relented. "There are good spirits and bad."

"Are you quite sure you can control them?" he asked.

"Oh, yes. Of course, we should go in together. Two against one."

He nodded.

I supposed that left me behind. I knew I was no sorceress, but after I had summoned the Queen, and helped Hollin fight the spirits before . . . didn't that show I had some ability? I didn't want to miss the look on Miss Rashten's face when she realized her day had come to an end, after the way she'd treated me.

"Is there anything I can do?" I asked. "My singing helped before. And my candle."

"Nimira, this is serious sorcery," Hollin said. "You'd get hurt."

"Nimira can help," Annalie said. "I can't bear the light of day. I'll need someone to guide me. It shouldn't be you, Hollin—you'll be busy enough fighting her off."

"Yes, I can do that." I smiled, for the first time in what seemed like an age. I think the truth of it all rushed in, when I thought of protecting Annalie in a fight. We would fight Miss Rashten. We would save Erris.

I dared not consider any other outcome.

29

We spent a little time forming a plan before Hollin went to fetch his sorcerer's staff and Annalie disappeared into her bedroom. I sipped at a cup of coffee, hoping I really could play some useful part in our escape.

Annalie emerged like a devout member of some modest religion. Black leather gloves disappeared up her draping sleeves. Her hood covered her neck, her ears, and her thick, dark hair. Just her face peered out, with her long lashes and her strong nose. She gave me a small smile, and said, "Miss Rashten might be frightened off by my appearance alone."

Over her face she drew a veil so thick I could no longer see her eyes, nor, I imagined, could she see mine.

She reached an arm out to me. "I put my trust in you, Nimira," she said.

I took her hand.

We watched the clock, waiting for Hollin to return.

"It doesn't take very long to walk to his bedroom," Annalie said, fidgeting a little. "I hope he's all right."

I'm sure her heart pounded, as mine did. Even if Hollin was about to open that door any moment, I had no idea what was ahead. We didn't know how much power Miss Rashten had, but I had a feeling sorcerer's battles were not quite like the ones in plays. I hoped Annalie really knew what she was doing.

I was just about to open the door to the next chamber when we heard a shout.

"That's Hollin!" Annalie tried to step forward, her outstretched arm seeking the wall, but I held her back.

"You'll hurt yourself! Take my arm—it's what I'm here for, isn't it?"

Her fingers found my shoulders and gripped there. She gave me a little shove. "Go, then. We have to help him."

I heard Rashten shouting now, and Hollin shouting over her. Something crashed. I heard Hollin yell, not the shout of spell-casting, but a cry of pain. I hurried forward, a few of Annalie's orbs still following, and opened the door. I peered out with one eye, and ducked back in when I saw Miss Rashten at the end of the hall with a long white sorcerer's staff. Her eye swept over me just before I pulled away.

"Did you see her?" Annalie whispered in my ear.

"*Yes.*"

Miss Rashten and Hollin kept crying out their incantations, all in that strange tongue of magic, where the words swept and rolled through the air like forces of nature in themselves.

Annalie whispered something under her breath, until a sound cut her off.

It sizzled, like a firework, and something streaked past my eyes, leaving blinding trails across my vision.

Lights.

Five lights swept into the room, not the gentle glowing lights that Annalie summoned, but lights that flashed and sparked. Instinctively, I stepped back, trodding on Annalie's skirt, and she was forced to hurry behind me until she hit the sofa with a cry. I swatted a light with my hand and it stung like a bee.

"Ow!"

"What is it?" Annalie whirled in place. The lights made faint whizzing sounds as they darted around us, and I could see her trying to avoid the sound. While I ducked to avoid one of them, two of the remaining lights rushed to her, one burning a hole through her skirt while the other aimed for her face.

"Duck!" I cried.

I quickly snatched a pillow from the sofa and swatted the light from the air. It left a hole like a cigarette burn. I turned, trying to find the other one, only to feel it sting my back.

I hit my back with the pillow, but too late, of course—the thing had found its mark.

"They're gone—for now," I said, gasping.

"What were they?"

"Lights. They burned a hole in your dress, but not your petticoat, looks like. One was going for your face. They burn when they touch." I glanced at the growing welt on my hand where I'd swatted the light away. "Try to summon your spirits." No sooner had I spoken than a fresh round of the whizzing lights streaked into the room, and I had to rush forward to fend them off before they hit Annalie.

I realized I hadn't heard Hollin in a while.

Miss Rashten called to us from the hall. "Are you keeping busy in there, girls? It's just the two of you now."

"Oh, *no*," Annalie said. She looked ready to run forward again. One of the lights took the distraction to jab me right in the cheek, the worst one of all. Tears leaped to my eyes.

The room was dark again, except for the three dancing orbs that had followed Annalie from her bedroom. They circled around the ceiling, keeping the room illuminated for me.

I kept looking for any stray lights, but I knew no more would come just yet. *She* would come now. It must have been just a handful of seconds that we waited there, but time grew slow and horrible. My mouth feared to make a peep. The same horrible thrall must have held Annalie.

Miss Rashten entered the doorway. I half expected her to have changed, to bear some demon's face, but she was the same wrinkled old woman, with the same old cap. My eyes traveled the length of her white staff, an elegant thing nearly as tall as she. It didn't seem to suit her.

"I'm sorry," she said. "But I warned you, Miss Nimira, didn't I?"

She struck her staff against the ground, and another dozen of the lights burst forth from the tip and rose up like the sparks from a fire, to circle around the staff's head. She gestured with the staff, and the lights flew to Annalie, swirling around her like a living net. Annalie's orbs floated nearby, bunched together at a cautious distance, as if plotting a rescue. I wished it were so!

"Annalie, don't move," I said. "Her lights are all around you."

"I knew you were all plotting some nonsense," Rashten said. "Hollin's down. Annalie, return to your room. Nimira, you come with me."

I wished I knew what to do. We had planned for Hollin to

distract Miss Rashten while Annalie summoned the spirits, but Miss Rashten had set her lights upon us almost from the start.

"I won't go to my room," Annalie said. "I'd rather you did kill me."

"Ridiculous." Miss Rashten touched my arm with the head of her staff. It burned, although not so much as her lights, and I managed not to react besides a tightening of muscles in my shoulders. "Come on," she said. "Come on . . . good girl, Miss Nimira."

Annalie had kept very still, hands at her sides. Miss Rashten's lights lifted from around her, returning to the staff.

"You can move now, Annalie," I said, trying to keep my voice steady. "Go back to your room; don't worry about me." I hoped Annalie would worry about me, and would do something, but I supposed my only chance of giving her time to summon the spirits was to deflect Miss Rashten's attention from her.

"Where are you taking her?" Annalie demanded. Miss Rashten was herding me from the room with the staff pointed at my back like a pistol. Annalie's fingers found the wall and she groped forward after us, her orbs following, staying near the ceiling.

"I'm sending her away," Miss Rashten said slowly. Every word was ominous. I knew she wouldn't just send me anywhere.

Annalie's orbs drew closer to her, and she reached for my arm, but Miss Rashten struck her across the face with the staff and she reeled back. I stamped on Rashten's foot and scrambled to find something I could use as a weapon, but the room was almost empty of adornment or function. Rashten had time to strike back, and strike she did. Her staff flared, releasing a force that knocked me against the wall. The pain came a moment later, filling my eyes with stars.

When my head cleared, Annalie had thrown back her veil

and was trying to wrest the staff from Miss Rashten's hands. She was cringing and squinting with pain from the light, but Rashten couldn't seem to control her staff as long as Annalie had hold of it. If only I had something I could use as a weapon!

No sooner had I mustered this thought than I saw two hands appear in the door, holding a pistol between them.

Linza.

"Lift . . . your . . . *hands*," she said to Miss Rashten, her voice shaking so much you could hardly understand her.

Miss Rashten turned sharply. *"What—?"*

"I c-c-can fire this . . . p-pistol . . . faster than you can . . . do magic," Linza managed. She was, admittedly, not a terribly intimidating figure, with her eyes wide as some funny jungle creature, and the pistol wobbling in her hands.

Miss Rashten made a little, incredulous laugh, and yanked the staff from Annalie's surprised hands while Linza—

I wasn't afraid to act.

I grabbed the pistol from Linza's hand, pointed it at Miss Rashten's leg, and pulled the trigger before I had time to think twice about it.

The bullet only grazed her leg, but she shrieked with pain. Now my hands were shaking as blood spots appeared on her dress. Although the pain still must have been terrific, she regained her composure quickly and lifted her staff.

"You move and I'll kill you," I said, pointing the pistol at her heart, or thereabouts. The voice coming from my mouth didn't sound like mine at all, but I let it go on. "If you try to hurt us again, I swear I'll shoot."

I held the pistol pointed at her, and she had the staff pointed at me, and someone had to make the first move.

I counted seconds in my head, fixing my eyes on her, afraid to blink.

Her lips crept into a smile. "You can't do it, can you?"

Two of Annalie's orbs drifted toward their mistress, I noticed from the corner of my eye, but I dared not take my attention off of Miss Rashten. If I could just keep her distracted long enough.

"I shot you already, didn't I?" I said.

"Put down the gun," she said. "You dare shoot me again, and this staff has enough power to take the whole lot of you with me."

I felt the trigger, potent beneath my finger. I could pull it and end this. Her threat about the power in the staff could be a bluff.

She was right, though. I didn't really want to deal death with my own hands.

Miss Rashten suddenly noticed the orbs fluttering around Annalie. Their number had increased noticeably, even brightening the room. "Hey now, what's this?" She thrust the staff at Annalie, but Annalie did not even look at her. She was lowering her veil and the orbs gathered around her shoulders, protectively it seemed.

Miss Rashten moved to strike her with the staff, but then she stopped and peered at the ceiling, like she'd heard someone calling.

And then I heard it, too. *Rashten Rashten . . . cursed traitor . . . fallen fallen . . .*

"What is that?" she said, and for the first time, she sounded truly nervous.

"My friends," Annalie said.

The room was beginning to fall into darkness. The light from the open hallway door was shrinking back.

Annalie faced Rashten. The orbs gathered behind her, casting soft illumination on the wall, while creating a silhouette out of her.

Her shadow ran a path to Miss Rashten, who lifted her staff like she meant to strike, once she figured out what to strike *at*.

Two forms melted from Annalie's shadow, taking on a certain smoky substance, with lanky arms and legs.

"She is the one you want," Annalie said, now holding her arm out like a general leading her army. With jerking movements, the shadow beings slid toward Miss Rashten. They had come to help us, but I think I was nearly as scared of them as she was.

They gathered around her, linking arms of liquid black, melding into one form that held her tight between them. She made shuddering cries, like she couldn't breathe.

The shadows had brought the frigid cold with them. I hurried to Annalie's side. She held a hand out to me, and I took it. My fingers shivered, and she squeezed them. "Let's go," she whispered. "They will handle her."

Miss Rashten thrust a hand out from the shadows. The darkness quickly pulled it back into its web. I saw only flashes of her cap or the hem of her skirt. The room had gone so dark. Linza was standing frozen with terror, and I grabbed her arm and pulled her from the room. She stumbled after me, while Annalie kept her arm about my waist.

Together, we left the room behind.

30

As Linza recovered her wits, she realized I was leading Annalie, and flanked her other side. Hand in hand, we picked up our pace. I felt a thrill of unity. We'd done it—Linza and Annalie and I together. I was so heady with adrenaline, I could have skipped down the stairs.

"Will they leave on their own?" I asked Annalie. "Or do you have to dismiss them?"

"They can depart without me," she said.

We found Hollin slumped in the hall like a napping laborer. He came to at the sound of our footsteps and struggled to his feet just as we swarmed him. Annalie's hands reached for his chest, his arm—whatever they found.

"Did she hurt you?" she asked.

"I'll be all right. Bruised, I'm sure. What—what happened? You're all right?" He put a hand to Annalie's shoulder, and then even mine. He looked like he wanted to grab the both of us close.

"Yes," Annalie said. "I think she is dead."

"Thank God," he breathed.

I said a silent prayer for Miss Rashten's soul, although truth be told, I didn't feel tremendously sorry.

"I'm sorry I was so useless," Hollin said. "She caught me coming back from my bedroom." He noticed the pistol in my hand. "How did you get my gun?"

"I did, sir," Linza said. "I'm sorry. I knew you kept a pistol near your bed. I'd seen it when I cleaned—I'm sorry." Her cheeks were flushed.

"Don't be sorry," Annalie said. "It was quick thinking."

"You shall certainly have a raise," Hollin said. "But now we must not waste any time. I'm going to make sure Miss Rashten is taken care of, and then we'll make haste to New Sweeling."

I had almost forgotten, in the rush of the moment, that besting Miss Rashten was only half the battle. Smollings still had Erris, and he might destroy him before we could save him.

∞∞∞

These same roads had once delivered me from my life as a trouser girl. Now I hoped they would bring me to a greater triumph, but nothing could be sure. I could hardly bear my own thoughts, but no one had much to say. Annalie wore her veil, and her orbs had all retreated. I supposed they weren't fond of travel. Hollin looked at her from the corner of his eye much of the time, a mixture of guilt and concern. I stared out the window and wondered how Erris fared.

We reached New Sweeling after nightfall. I half expected to find the city in an expectant hush, but of course it was just another night, with music spilling from taverns and nightclubs, gaslights illuminating urchins selling songsheets and matches, theatergoers in fur wraps and fine suits strolling to their carriages.

Our carriage slowed before a grand apartment of twelve or so stories, *The Aubrey*.

We walked up to the double doors. Their elegant stained glass panes depicted lilies and reeds, in the very latest style. Two narrow rows of clear windows framed the doors, and through them we saw the night watchman, sitting at the lobby desk.

Hollin tried the door, but it was locked. He knocked, and then poked his face in the clear windows. The night watchman came and stared at him for a moment.

"Let us in! I need to see Karstor Greinfern!"

The door opened. The night watchman looked somewhat flustered. "He's not expecting anyone."

"It's Hollin Parry," Hollin said, flashing his card. "I'm sure he'll want to see me."

The man still looked unsure, but he admitted us. After a brief call up to Karstor, we took the elevator to the topmost floor, where Karstor, clad in slippers and dressing gown, was already waiting for us.

"Hollin Parry?" His eyes darted between the three of us. "What's going on? What is this?"

"A rescue mission," Hollin said. "And . . . an apology."

❧ 31 ❧

Karstor invited us in and showed us into a parlor cluttered with classical statues, heavy furniture, and musical instruments. His home smelled of mildly burned baked goods. I led Annalie forward.

"Have you received a summons for a meeting of council?" Hollin asked Karstor.

"The council meets tomorrow, in fact," Karstor replied. "Why?"

"Good. I don't think Smollings knows we're here." He glanced back at us. "Dr. Greinfern, do you mind if we turn off the lights? They bother my wife."

"Your wife?" Karstor furrowed his dark brows. "You don't mean . . . little Anni?"

"Yes, Dr. Greinfern." Annalie extended a hand toward him. "It's me. If you don't mind, I can remove my veil if you turn off your lights. The moon doesn't bother me so very much."

He took her hand and briefly placed his other hand atop it in greeting, then switched off the lamp. The moon still left the room bright enough to see.

"You do look just like your father, only pretty, I think," Karstor said as she lifted the veil from her face. She smiled, but Hollin looked impatient.

"Sit down," he said. "I have a lot to say and the hour is already late."

Karstor nodded and *hmm*ed as we explained how Annalie still lived and why Smollings had wanted to keep her secret as much as Hollin did, about my summoning of the Lady, and Smollings taking Erris. It was not until the end, when Hollin told Karstor that Smollings had killed Garvin, that he gripped the arms of his chair and lost his composure.

"How do you know?"

"I know, Dr. Greinfern," Annalie said, "because Garvin's spirit has visited me and told me so."

"Is his spirit here now?"

"Yes." Annalie looked at the orbs floating around her and put out a silencing hand to us. "Yes," she repeated.

Hollin was fidgeting in his chair, unnerved as ever by Annalie's ability to speak to spirits.

"Oh— Oh, God." Karstor took a deep breath. "It was Garvin's dream to restore the throne of the lost fairy prince. When I opened the letter telling me he had found an automaton with Erris's spirit inside, I thought my heart would stop. But it sounds as if Smollings was plotting his death before he even knew about Erris." He shook his head. "Doomed before he started."

"It's not too late to fulfill his dream," I said, burying the thought that placing Erris on the fairy throne might take him away from me.

"We all have business with Smollings now." Hollin laced his fingers. "He killed Garvin, he's taken Nimira's fairy prince, and he's forced me to keep my wife a captive in her own home. God willing, I don't think it's too late to save us all. But we'll need your help, Dr. Greinfern."

For a moment, Karstor's eyes followed the orbs dancing around Annalie's head. "Anything I can do," he said, "for an old friend."

After a poor sleep and a rich breakfast, choked down under the eye of Karstor's enthusiastic cook, we rode through New Sweeling's finest district to Sorcerer's Hall, where the council held their meetings. Government buildings lined the entire street, with the clock tower of the capitol standing sentry over them all. The hall was compact but elegant, made of tawny bricks, and gilt adornments on the roof gleamed in the sun. Two men in sharp government uniforms holding sorcerer's staffs guarded the doors.

I wondered if Smollings was already here. Was Erris in the building now?

"Half an hour?" Karstor asked Annalie.

We planned to stay in the carriage while Karstor entered the council meeting. While Karstor questioned Smollings, trying to set up for our entrance, Annalie would make contact with Garvin's spirit.

"If you can't get past the guards, just make as much commotion as possible to draw our attention," Karstor said. He looked out the carriage window. "There he is."

Smollings was walking up to the doors, speaking to a plump sorcerer with ample sideburns. No sign of Erris.

"I'd feel much better if we were allowed to bring our staffs inside," Hollin said.

Karstor snorted. "I do think we'd all have killed each other by now if that were permitted." He checked his pocket watch. "Well, good luck."

"Same to you," Hollin replied.

"Wait," I said. "I—I—could I come with you?" I had agreed to wait in the carriage before, but seeing Smollings again, knowing Erris might be in the building now, I couldn't bear it. "I have to know if Erris is all right."

"No," Hollin said. "You'll disturb the plan."

"But how? Smollings will just think I gave you the slip and found Karstor—er, Dr. Greinfern on my own, and now Dr. Greinfern is bringing me to the council to present my side of the story. Right?" I looked at Karstor hopefully, and to my relief, he nodded.

"We don't have time to argue," he said. "I know how it feels to wonder if someone you care for is alive or dead. Come with me."

Smollings and the plump sorcerer had disappeared through the doors. Karstor left the carriage first, then offered me a hand. Hollin seemed very tense, and I wondered if he had argued for me to stay so he wouldn't be left alone with Annalie while she summoned Garvin's spirit.

We weren't halfway up the stairs when a stone-faced guard stepped forward to bar our way with his sorcerer's staff. The other guard slipped through the doors. "I'm sorry, Dr. Greinfern, but I'm sure you know it's a council meeting today. Your company will have to wait outside."

"She's with me," Karstor said. "I have business with the council, very important, and she's part of that business."

"Ambassador Smollings explicitly reminded us that the rules do not allow anyone to attend council without proper authorization."

The doors opened again. Smollings emerged behind the other guard, and if he was surprised by my presence, he didn't show it.

"Well, Dr. Greinfern, what fascinating company you keep."

Karstor stared at Smollings. He merely stared. He didn't say a word. He didn't even seem to be breathing. The guards shifted uncomfortably, for it looked very much as if Karstor was about to grab Smollings by the neck and strangle him right there on the stairs of Sorcerer's Hall.

"Well," Smollings said. "Look, you can't bring her in."

"She is not company," Karstor said. "She is evidence. Evidence of treason, Mr. Smollings. And I have every right by law to present *that* to the council."

"Treason!" Smollings shook his head. "My goodness. I shall be interested to see if this trouser girl's affection for that machine has anything to do with such an idea."

The guard permitted us to cross the threshold, and as we entered the council room, I spotted Erris at once. But it was not Erris as I had known him. His arms and torso had been stripped of skin. He was metal and gears. A toy. A dead thing. His face and hands were still as I had known and touched them, but his eyes were closed, his mouth slack. I clapped my hand to my mouth, suppressing a shriek.

Karstor took my arm and turned me around so I couldn't see him, but I was still making some terrible whimpering sound, and I felt the eyes of a roomful of sorcerers upon me.

"I apologize for the shock," Smollings said. "I removed the automaton's clothes. Some members of the council wished to inspect his mechanism."

"*He had skin!*" The scream ripped from my throat. "What did you do to him?"

The sorcerers were murmuring. Smollings lifted his arm with a flourish. "Well, miss! And how is it you know this? Had you ... *disrobed* the automaton?"

Someone chuckled.

"No! No, but—he was alive!" I spoke through sobs. "I just—I knew!" It was true, I never had seen Erris beneath his clothes, aside from where the keyhole showed in his back, but I had held his arm, embraced him, touched his hands. He had thought himself brought fully to life until his mechanism wound down. He must have ...

But now I wasn't entirely sure.

"I'm getting ahead of myself," Smollings said. "Let us officially convene. I gathered you all here to present the interesting story of this automaton, and I do believe this girl may support my theory. She, in fact, has been living in Hollin Parry's house, where I found the automaton." He pointed at a chair next to the one that held Erris ... or his body, at least. "Please. Sit down."

I took the chair, for I didn't see how I could refuse it. I struggled to regain my composure. I must not let Smollings have any more of his desired reaction.

Oh, but how my lips *would* tremble. And how my heart would break!

"Some of you may have heard the rumor, that a prince of the House of Tanharrow still lived, trapped in the body of an automaton."

As Smollings told the council of his suspicions, I had a moment to muster my courage. I had fought for Erris before. He didn't look truly dead, just unwound. Annalie would summon Garvin.

Breathe . . .

"When I heard Mr. Parry had purchased the automaton from Garvin Pelerine's estate, it roused my interest, for I had never heard Mr. Pelerine express an interest in automata. I paid Parry a visit, and although he denied anything unusual, I heard this girl speaking with the automaton. Parry and the girl later managed, through forbidden contact with the underworld, to bring the automaton to a kind of grotesque life."

"This automaton is the fairy prince?" the plump sorcerer asked, although I suspected he already knew the story by the smug expression on his face. "Well, what did Mr. Pelerine intend to do with him? He should have turned him over to the council immediately."

"That is exactly my question," Smollings said. He slipped his hand beneath his black vest and took out Erris's key.

I squirmed in my chair as Smollings walked behind Erris and inserted the key in his back. I imagined that key grinding in my own spine. I wanted to do something to spare Erris from the moment to come, but a terrible paralysis seized me.

Erris began to tick. It was not a loud sound, but I heard it like a far-off cry for help. The sorcerers quieted their murmuring.

Smollings didn't take the key out. He kept his fingers on it while it turned.

Erris opened his eyes. His expression was pure shock, seeing all the sorcerers with their pointed cuffs and serious expressions, sitting at their heavy wooden tables.

And me. Our eyes met, and my nostrils flared with the effort of not crying, and Erris looked down at his arms and chest. The slow turning of the metallic drum was visible through the armature.

He let out a small horrified sound that echoed in the room.

Smollings loomed behind him, cold and hard as the face of a rock. "What is your name?" he asked.

I wondered if Erris had even heard. He seemed lost. He wouldn't look at me anymore, but I couldn't stop looking at him, although I would have torn out my own eyes not to see him so pained.

Smollings made a jerking motion, twisting the key, and Erris started to fall. He snapped up again when Smollings let go, a look of shock on his face. "What is your name?" he asked again.

"Erris!"

Smollings could turn Erris off and on at will. And he was hurting him. Could he break?

"Erris what?"

"Erris Tanharrow."

"Did you know Garvin Pelerine?"

A pause. Another twist of the key. Erris gasped, like a drowning man fighting to keep above the waves. *"Yes."*

I couldn't bear another moment of this. I shot to my feet. "You're hurting him!" I screamed. I hardly even thought about the sorcerers anymore, or anything except the fury that raced through me. "Stop! You *stop!*"

"I suspect the girl has inconceivably fallen in love with the automaton," Smollings said. "She risked her life, indeed the lives of everyone in Mr. Hollin Parry's house, to free him. Finishing a job that I believe Garvin Pelerine began. What did Garvin intend to do with you?" he asked Erris.

"I—I don't know."

"He didn't speak of restoring you to the throne?"

"I don't want the throne!" Erris shouted.

A nervous-looking man stood up, smoothing the front of his

suit. "But . . . if this is true . . . Many fairies have yet to give up hope that the House of Tanharrow might be restored. What would this mean for us?"

"I'm not sure yet," Smollings said. "All I know is that Mr. Pelerine was communicating with this—thing, this . . . fairy prince, and he told no one . . . except, perhaps, Dr. Greinfern."

"I did notice Dr. Greinfern took an interest in the automaton at Aldren Hall," said a blond man with neatly parted hair and a mustache.

Smollings twitched Erris's key again, provoking another gasp. "Tell us, Dr. Greinfern. Please."

Karstor stood, his eyes shooting fury at Smollings. "Yes. I knew. I was in Heinlede, but Garvin wrote me. He had only just discovered the automaton and suspected he was the lost prince. I'm sure he meant to tell the council, once he was sure of what he had, but then he rather conveniently *died*."

"Oh, yes," said Smollings. "You brought this girl because you had some far-fetched idea about . . . treason, was it? Please, Miss Nimira, let's hear it."

"I—I—that is—" They were all looking at me, the sorcerers, with suspicious or incredulous faces. They didn't want to believe a word I said.

"Very impressive," the blond sorcerer quipped. "Perhaps the little savage can't find the words in our language."

"If I can't find the words, it's because there aren't words nasty enough in your language!" Damn it all, what did I have to lose anyway? "I'm not the savage. *Mr. Smollings* is the savage. He killed Garvin Pelerine, and he keeps Annalie Parry a captive!"

"That's ridiculous," the plump sorcerer said. "Annalie Parry? Hollin Parry's wife? But didn't she die a little while back?"

He stopped. The doors were opening. Annalie entered, without her hood, so her hair flowed down her back. Her body seemed lit from within, her eyes a queer blue instead of brown. She was almost terrifying. Hollin entered behind her, rather like an afterthought.

"I am here," she said, with a voice so resonant that it sounded like two voices speaking at once.

The plump man sputtered. "Isn't—isn't that Annalie Parry now?"

"I am Annalie Parry," she said. "I am also Garvin Pelerine. Two souls, in one body, for this moment, so we might tell the truth." She stalked forward until she stood between the two council tables. "Let go of the key, Smollings. Now."

Smollings dropped his hand from the key and stepped back. "You're not Garvin," he said.

"Oh, but I am. You *know* where I came from. You have used this girl, Annalie Parry, to speak to the spirits—*dark* spirits—many times. You must have known I would be waiting for you. You thought you could manipulate Hollin Parry because he lived in fear of the council's reaction if it was discovered that he had conjured the spirit world to save her. . . . And for a while, I despaired that you were right."

Hollin stood quite still. His gaze had dropped, and now it traveled down the center aisle, toward Smollings—no, toward me. Our eyes met, and I'm not sure I could explain what was exchanged. Was he apologizing? Was he drawing strength from my support? Maybe he only wanted final confirmation that he was making the right decision.

You are.

Hollin spoke then. "I will attest to it. My wife, Annalie, didn't die of the fever. I tried to save her life using forbidden necromancy. My attempt left her weak, and the spirits seemed to possess her. It also left her able to communicate with the dead. When I told Mr. Smollings, my father's old friend, he told me he'd cover up my crime, but it was clear he had a motive. Ever since then, he has used my wife to tap into dark magic himself."

The sorcerers were whispering amongst themselves, and even the ones that had insulted me or expressed suspicions about Garvin now seemed nervous. Annalie was so striking, and she spoke with such conviction, that Smollings had lost his poise the moment she arrived.

Now I could see him fighting to regain it. "And why should we believe you're Garvin Pelerine? You could tell us you're anyone, but I see no proof. You're trying to frame *me* for what Hollin Parry did."

"You're pale, Smollings," Annalie said. "As pale and shocked as I must have looked when you ambushed me that day in the forest. I knew we'd never agree on the fairies or much of anything else, but I couldn't believe you'd kill a man over politics. You obviously planned this a long time—you anticipated every spell in my repertoire. Since you know me so well, ask me anything, and I'll tell you. I can tell you, Mr. Fidinch"—she indicated the plump man—"once we were at lunch, discussing griffon hunting laws, and we had a very buxom waitress you had taken a shine to . . ."

"That's enough," Fidinch said, getting quite red.

"Exactly," Annalie said. "What about you, Melsing? I have some stories of our school days I'd be happy to share."

Melsing held up a hand for Annalie—Garvin—to halt.

"But I also know your sorrows and your hearts," Annalie said. "Those of you that have them." She looked at the blond man.

"When your boy was so ill, Mr. Favier, I sat up with you, distracting you, talking of philosophy and pastries."

"It *is* Garvin," Mr. Favier said. "She might look like Annalie Parry, but she *talks* like Garvin."

No one seemed to notice Smollings taking out the pistol. I didn't notice myself, until I heard chair legs screech, and saw Erris launch himself at Smollings and seize him from behind.

The pistol fired, striking not Annalie, but Karstor, who lurched backward, clutching his shoulder, knocking into his chair before slumping to the ground.

"Karstor!" Annalie cried, swooping to his side.

Erris kept his grip on Smollings, who had gone strangely limp.

Hollin reached inside his own jacket and pointed his pistol at Smollings. "Drop your weapon."

Smollings opened his hand. The pistol fell. A queer smile slashed across his face.

"I hope you're happy, Parry," Smollings said. "You've secured a victory for that which is dark and godless. I see the door closing on Lorinar's golden age. At least I can say *I* fought to the last."

I sensed hesitancy in the room. No one wanted to cheer for Smollings—not at this moment—but some eyes were suspicious. Some hearts agreed. Moments ago, the sorcerers had been under Smollings's thumb.

"It's only his shoulder," said one of the sorcerers who had knelt to help Karstor. "But he needs a doctor."

Annalie stood, obviously reluctant to take her attention from Karstor. Her breath came heavy. "You're wrong, Smollings," she said. "Lorinar's golden age is just beginning. What you call our golden age has been a time of war and intolerance. It isn't the place of mere men to judge who is godless, but rather, our duty to be the world's keepers and protectors—a job at which we have, thus far, failed."

She took a step back, clutching her head. "I can't stay much longer . . ." She dropped to her knees. Karstor struggled to rise.

"Greinfern, don't, you're injured!" said the sorcerer who had been tending to him.

"I have to say good-bye!" He touched Annalie's back. "Hang on, old friend. Hang on. Don't go, don't leave me."

"I have to go . . . ," Garvin whispered with Annalie's voice. "It has taken great effort, for me and for Annalie Parry, to be here today. You must stay . . . help our country find a peaceful resolution with the fairies . . . I know you have it in you." Annalie's hands reached for Karstor, drawing his ear to her, where she whispered something.

Karstor's eyes welled.

"Good-bye," Annalie said. The luminous presence that had entered seemed to retreat, and she became Annalie of the shadows again, drawing her hood over her hair with one slender, trembling arm.

Karstor clutched his wound, obviously in pain as he shuddered with soundless grief.

The doors burst open. The police stormed into the room, their coat buttons gleaming. Someone must have called them.

"Please, everyone—stay seated," one of the policemen shouted, in vain.

A number of the police were halted in their tracks, staring at Erris. "What—what is this thing?"

My ears burned to hear it—like he had no name. This was the man I loved! *This thing.*

Even I had to admit, it was hard to see his humanity through all the exposed clockwork. I didn't know if he could be fixed. But behind the gears and metal, I saw his soul, vibrant and living. For one precious moment, it all melted away, and I remembered the words of the Queen of the Longest Night when she had told me to take care of Erris. *You have all the strength you need.*

"He isn't a thing," I said. "He's Erris." And I took his hand.

32

Erris was neither human nor fairy, and all my love could not change that fact.

Smollings's home was searched that evening, but they found no evidence of skin, and even if they had, how would we have reattached it? The illusion of life was broken.

"It was just . . . a glamour," Erris told me, looking very serious. It was late by this time, and the day had been an exhausting round of police questioning and confusion. We had our first moment alone in a room of the massive New Sweeling police station.

"How does a glamour work?"

"An animation spell gives this body life . . . but the glamour tricks us into believing I'm real again. I know what fairy magic is capable of. We might be able to find a sorcerer to put up the illusion again, but . . ."

Panic scattered my thoughts. He would want to leave me. He wouldn't want to live like this. "What can we do?"

He squeezed my hands. He was dressed in a suit again. He looked like anyone else. "I really don't know. I'm not going to do anything rash . . ." Erris made a fairly ineffective attempt at a reassuring smile.

A policeman opened the door, admitting Karstor. His wound, thankfully, had been largely superficial.

"You're both free to go," Karstor said. "You can come home with me."

"We are?" Erris said. The prospect of freedom seemed almost to frighten him.

"You have diplomatic immunity, Mr. Tanharrow," Karstor said. "We can't just hold a member of the fairy royal family. Come on. I imagine you both need rest. Later we'll discuss what the next step will be. I'm sure you want to go home, but even that is hardly a simple matter with a king already on the throne."

"What about Hollin and Annalie?" I asked, rising to walk with him.

"Hollin's punishment will not be terribly severe," Karstor said. "In light of the circumstances." He looked at us, quite serious. "After Smollings, I have the highest rank on the council. I'm the Ambassador of Magic now. Not a responsibility I expected to inherit this quickly, if ever."

"I know how you feel," Erris said.

Karstor nodded.

A carriage brought us back to Karstor's elegant apartment, where the well-intentioned cook plied us with baked goods the moment we sat down. This was not a house like most, where a maid brought food out from the mysterious realms of the kitchen. Karstor's cook, apron-clad and dusted with flour, proudly displayed a towering pile of apple tarts and slender slices of chocolatey things topped with lattice and powdered sugar.

"Thank you, Birte," Karstor said rather absently, sinking into his chair. He spoke to her in what must have been their native tongue, something kind but dismissive.

"You eat and you will feel better," she said, lifting a tart onto a plate, and placing it on his lap whether he liked it or not. She clearly intended to serve Erris next.

"No, thank you," Erris said.

"It's very good," she said. "I know you'll feel better also. People say my tarts are as good as magic."

"I can't *eat*," he said.

"Once you taste it—" She put another tart on a plate.

"Birte, he means it," Karstor. "I'll explain later."

As she bustled from the room, Erris buried his face in his hands.

"Erris—," I began.

"There is nothing to say." He got to his feet and rushed to the bedrooms, and I felt so powerless. I could fight dark spirits for him, fight Smollings for him . . . but even I couldn't fight this.

"He needs time to grieve," Karstor said, probably speaking of himself as much as Erris.

I reached for a tart, and hoped they really were magic.

———

As one day passed, and then another, I tried to smile and say reassuring things whenever we spent time together. Karstor urged us to play cards, he offered books, he even gave us tickets for the theater, which neither of us had the slightest desire to use. He turned away everyone who wished to speak with us. I think we had some delusion that if we never left the apartment and never talked of plans, time would stop and decisions could be avoided.

But I could never forget what Erris was. Every morning, I wound him. I didn't want to wind him; I feared he would start to resent me. But someone had to do it, and better myself than any other.

I felt awful when he caught me crying on my bed, my head pressed into my pillow.

"Don't be sad," he said.

I summoned up my false smile. I'd been making good use of it. "I'm not."

"I was thinking, I should give you a concert," he said. "I haven't played a real song in years and years. I see Karstor has a piano."

"Oh, I would love to hear you play."

The piano was tucked into a cozy corner in a room full of books. Erris picked up a chair from the side of the room and plopped it in the center of the rug, facing the piano.

"Have a seat, milady."

I sat, arranged my skirts, and folded my hands expectantly. Erris took the piano bench, flipping his coat out behind him.

I had always loved music for the way it heightened my emotions and lifted the veil to other worlds. As Erris played, his music grew more bold and strange, and he started to lose himself in it. He might have forgotten I was there, with such intensity he played.

This, then, was fairy music. I think I understood what fairies were, for the first time: not the tricksters or the dainty creatures of Lorinar's tales, but people tied to the earth. In Erris's melodies I heard the slow strength of trees, the fragility of flowers, and the ache of dreams. He carried me into them, and showed me where he had come from, as much as any picture or story.

Erris finally sat back, blinking slowly at the ceiling.

"Erris, that was beautiful."

"I'm out of practice," he said. "But I've missed it more than I knew." I heard something new in his voice—a desire for the music he had missed. Maybe even for the land he had left behind. I was glad. If he was to stay with me, he would need something more to live for.

I went to stand beside him. He clasped my hand against his shoulder.

The door was open, but Karstor still knocked on the frame before he entered.

"A letter for you, Nimira," he said, holding it out.

"It's from Hollin," I said, breaking the seal with my thumb. I read aloud.

Dear Nimira,

The opportunity to travel was the first desire of my youth, and to become a sorcerer the second, but my taste for magic has dimmed somewhat, in light of recent events. I have agreed to a yearlong position in New Guinnell, a Lorinarian colony rife with heat, insects, and adventure. They need sorcerers of my caliber to keep the region stable and explore new territory—and local forms of magic. I'll help our government in lieu of the usual penalty for using forbidden magic.

Annalie is going home to Vestenveld. It's what she wants, so don't worry for either of us. We've agreed that maybe time apart is what we need. She urges you to visit whenever you wish.

There is more, however. You and Erris have been ever on her mind. She has been spending every free hour in communication with the spirit world, and they have given her a message. There is a sorcerer named Ordorio Valdana—indeed, I have heard of him, and I am sure Dr. Greinfern will know his name as well. He was once on the council, one of the greatest necromancers of the last century, but after the war he became a recluse. No one knew why.

The spirits told Annalie he was once married, to a fairy woman, Melia Tanharrow. Erris's sister.

If anyone knows how to help Erris, it might be Mr. Valdana. He lives near the fairy gate, in the northern mountains. I hope you can find answers there.

Nimira, I'm sorry I drew you into the tangled web that has been my life these past couple years, but I must thank you for helping me to do what I did. When I was surrounded by falseness, yours was the voice of truth that helped me find my own. I wish you all the best.

Sincerely,
A. Hollin Parry

"Valdana! Yes," Karstor said. "I met him once, when I was just a student. He came to the academy. A rare sort of man, with such power you could nearly see it rising from him like smoke."

"And he was married to flighty old Mel?" Erris said.

I folded the letter with the slightest sigh. I hoped Hollin would find the adventure he'd hoped for in New Guinnell. I wished he could have had a happier ending with Annalie. As misguided as his actions often were, I knew it had all started with his love for her. Maybe a year abroad would be what he needed to heal.

"What do you think, Erris?" I asked. "Should we go find Mr. Valdana? I'd like to see mountains again."

"I think, Nim, that you should pack your coat," said Erris. "There could be hope for us yet."

✄ Acknowledgments ✄

My name might be on the cover of *Magic Under Glass*, but I couldn't have done without the following fabulous individuals:

Dade Bell, not just the love of my life but my political history advisor, sounding board, and the guy who listened to me read every single draft of this novel aloud. Fact: some of the best ideas in my stories are actually his.

My parents, for their love and trust in me and in radical education methods that allowed me a great deal of creative freedom. And to Mom for writing down my stories before I could write. Telling you both my book sold was a great moment.

My agent, Jennifer Laughran, for being lightning-fast, funny, and an all-around super agent. Yay!

My editors, Melanie Cecka and Sarah Odedina, for editing suggestions so fantastic that sometimes I thought my mind was being read and improved upon, and the rest of the Bloomsbury team.

Kate Dolamore, for years of complicated and fabulous pretend games and for just being a great sister.

Sarah Cross, for sending me a list of agents back in 2005 and ordering me to send a query out, already!

My beta readers, some dating back over three years and some who read more than once: Memory Arnould, Heather Cress, Liz Parker Garcia, Rose Green, Emily Hainsworth, Karen Kincy, Jackson Pearce, Robin Prehn, Rick Silva, and Jen "Awesome" VonDrak (who once sent me a supportive e-mail right when I really really needed it).

Sarah Hamilton, for being a lifeline for my imagination during the dark days of retail.

Freddie Baer, my fairy thriftmother, for boxes of clothes you better believe I'll wear to signings.

The children's writer community on Livejournal and around the Web. I wish I could add at least fifty more names here. So many have you have helped me, supported me, and made me laugh and think over the years.

And last but not least, all my dear family, friends, and coworkers who never laughed when I told them I wanted to be a writer.

Thank you, all.

Read on for a sneak peek at Jaclyn Dolamore's new novel

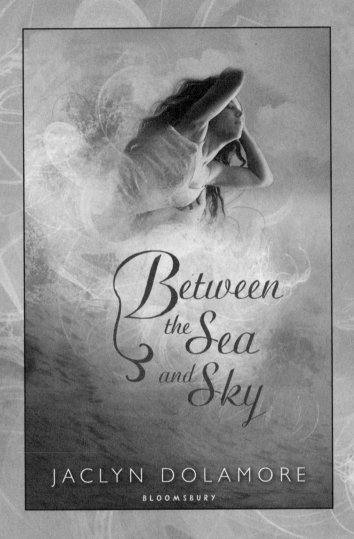

Between
the Sea
and Sky

JACLYN DOLAMORE

BLOOMSBURY

A GIRL FROM THE WATER
A BOY FROM THE AIR
A ROMANCE ON LAND

BLOOMSBURY
www.bloomsburyteens.com

1

It was not every day that a mermaid became a siren, and not every day that Esmerine attended such a party. It seemed just yesterday she had moped at home while her older sister, Dosinia, had spent the week in a whirlwind of ceremony and celebration for her siren's debut. Now Esmerine's turn had come.

"Yes, this is Esmerine, my second to oldest." Esmerine's mother put her arm around her daughter for perhaps the fiftieth time that evening.

"Well!" The older merwoman, her neck laden with pearls, made a slight dip. "Congratulations, Mrs. Lornamend—"

"Lorre*men*," her mother corrected. Everyone knew of the Lornamend merchant family, but the Lorremens were fishermen, and their name was hardly on the lips of society. "You may remember that my eldest daughter, Dosinia, was granted a siren's belt two years ago."

"Oh, of *course*," the older woman said. "Miss Dosinia, yes. She's a lovely young woman."

"Esmerine here is the brain of the family," Esmerine's mother continued. "She has a wonderful head for remembering songs and histories."

Esmerine smiled dutifully. Dosinia—Dosia to her sisters—was the pretty one, while she was the brain, and if they ever forgot, their mother would surely remind them.

The old woman paused in thought, her rather short tail gently waving. "Wasn't it one of your daughters who used to play with that little winged boy?" She frowned at Esmerine a little, disapproving the behavior even before it was confirmed.

"Oh, goodness, that was years ago! I had quite forgotten," her mother said, clearly a lie, for Esmerine was still teased about her friendship with Alander from time to time. She hadn't seen him in years, but the fact that she used to play with him, and worse—that he had taught her to read—had branded her as peculiar.

"I'm glad he doesn't come around anymore," the old woman continued. "Those people ought to keep a better eye on their children." She gave Esmerine's mother a pointed look, as if she should have done so herself.

"Excuse me," Esmerine said, catching Dosia's eye across the room. She swam upward with a flick of her tail.

Esmerine barely saw her sister these days. Even if Esmerine hadn't been busy preparing for her siren's initiation, Dosia was almost never home. Esmerine suspected she had a new beau.

Dosia stopped munching on olives long enough to wrap her arms around Esmerine's shoulders. "Finally!" Dosia squealed in her ear. They had been wishing all their lives to do something truly exciting together, and now that day had come. They would both be sirens.

Esmerine reached for an olive, glancing around for a server. "Where'd you get those?" she asked Dosia.

"They were just passing them out a minute ago. I'll share. They've got almonds inside." Dosia gave half her olives to Esmerine. Esmerine's mother only bought olives when good company was expected, complaining all the while about giving the traders a whole fish for a paltry handful of the surface-world treat.

"Don't tell me you're tired of trailing Mother around and meeting all those charming old rich ladies?" Dosia said with a grin.

"My favorite part," Esmerine said. "They keep calling us *Lornamends.*"

Dosia groaned. "I remember the same thing from my initiation, and I think they only do it so we're forced to correct them. Well, it doesn't matter, the rest of the sirens are lovely. This is the only night you have to endure these old matrons." Dosia made a face as a gentleman mer brushed by, his numerous strands of shell jewelry almost catching in her hair.

"Let's go up near the ceiling until the ceremony," Esmerine said. "It's so crowded here." Most of the mers had gathered at the bottom of the room, clinging to sculpted rocks or clustering by the floating lanterns.

"I thoroughly agree." Dosia grabbed Esmerine's arm and swished her tail, drawing them both up along the gently tapering walls. She stopped at a rock that jutted out not far from where water-freshening bubbles from an underground air pocket flowed through an opening in the ceiling. Although the bubbles occasionally obscured the view below, they had the space to themselves.

"So where have you been these past couple of weeks?" Esmerine asked. "I've hardly seen you."

"You've just been busy," Dosia said. "I've been around."

Esmerine raised her brows. "Hardly. And I haven't seen much of Jarra either." Dosia was always coy when a boy first caught her interest, but it was no secret that she had favored Jarra at dances lately.

Dosia paused, looking back toward the bottom of the room, where the water churned with movement. "Jarra?" She shook her head. "I haven't seen him either."

"Well, then, who?"

"Maybe I'm not interested in a *boy*," Dosia said. She looked embarrassed, which was odd for her.

The soft orbs of magic lights dimmed, signaling that the show would begin soon. The siren's ceremony would follow, and Esmerine knew she ought to take her place with Lady Minnaray in preparation, but she preferred to watch with Dosia.

The lights snuffed. Esmerine could hardly see Dosia's face. The eerie sound of female voices rose from the seafloor. Three merwomen appeared, pushing a softly glowing rock as tall as their length into the center of the floor.

Additional magical lights floated down through the opening in the ceiling, briefly illuminating Dosia's face as they passed. Mermen with their tails formed into legs and dressed in tattered clothes kicked their way down from the skylight. Behind them followed pairs of mermen, bearing white sails to represent the ship the humans rode.

The song of the women on the floor had faded, and now the men began to sing, mimicking the sea chanteys of human sailors. *If the winds hold fair we'll catch that whale, and if our luck is true, boys, we'll catch a mermaid too . . .*

As they sang, the rock on the floor cracked down the middle, releasing a narrow beam of light. The mermaid singers pried the rock open, revealing a mermaid nestled in a crystal lining, her rare red hair floating about her. Strands of tiny glowing beads ran through her hair, and a faux golden siren's belt glinted around her narrow waist.

O sisters, what handsome voice crept into my slumbering ear and brought to me a waking dream? The mermaid's pure, powerful voice put Esmerine's neighborhood singing club to shame.

One of the "human" men swam down, lured by her song. They locked eyes, and she began to drift toward him.

Sister, no! Come back! sang the mermaid chorus.

The other sirens pulled at her arms and fins, and she shook her head like she knew she'd been a fool, but in another moment she began to drift up again. The siren and the human man grew ever more enraptured by one another, until finally he slid her belt from her waist and she fainted dramatically into his arms, her tail splitting into legs with one final convulsion. The mermen bearing sails scattered around them while the sirens fled to a dark corner, cooing a sad song for the one they had lost. The merman actor did a magnificent job of portraying a human struggling to drag the mermaid's body to shore.

Dosia and Esmerine sighed at the romance and the tragedy to come. They knew this story well. Not a week went by when even the poorest merfolk didn't gather in homes and taverns to share songs and stories of their history.

As the next act began, the human man brought the siren to his home. Props brought from shipwrecks formed the stage set. She tried to please her new husband, but tongues of black "flame" from the seaweed fireplace burned her and she shied back from his horse—played by a muscular merman wearing a sea horse mask. Her husband finally lost patience, striking her across the face. The audience booed him with a passion.

"Humans aren't really like that," Dosia whispered.

"As if you've met one," Esmerine said. Dosia could be a real know-it-all about humans sometimes.

Dosia grinned. "I'd never be so stupid if I was a human's wife."

"I'd *love* to ride a horse," Esmerine said.

Dosia squeezed Esmerine's hand. "Me too."

In a final bid to win her husband's love, the siren confessed she was with child. His hand paused, midstrike, and suddenly he broke into a song of love, demonstrating his poor human values. Esmerine couldn't stand such moralistic tales, but of course the village elders hoped to scare the young sirens away from humans.

The lights dimmed as the stagehands cleared the props away. The somber opera of human cruelty and siren folly was followed by a trio of mermen who sang familiar comedic songs.

"We learned these in the nursery," Dosia scoffed.

"They can't get too bawdy, not with all these old ladies sponsoring it."

"Still, the Fish Song? They might as well not even bother."

One of the singing mermen noticed them talking and sang precisely in Dosia's direction, flourishing with an arm. Dosia huddled even closer to Esmerine.

"Oh *no*," she groaned.

"Don't even look at them anymore," said Esmerine.

"I won't. Anyway, you should probably find Lady Minnaray."

It was almost time for her siren's initiation. Esmerine hadn't allowed herself to think much of it, and her stomach had been in such a constant state of anxiety during the last few days that she had grown used to it. Being a siren was a great honor, an exalted place in mer society. No reason to be nervous, Lady Minnaray told her, but new initiates always were.

The possibilities of childhood—that she might grow up to be

an actress or a human pirate or a fisherwoman—had always been a game and an illusion, Esmerine realized. Her world was here. Nonetheless, it was scary to think of reciting the siren's pledge in front of everyone she knew and commit to one life forever.

She approached Lady Minnaray shyly. The eldest siren was tanned and wrinkled from a lifetime of sitting on the rocks, and she had a regal bearing despite her small size.

"You look lovely, Esmerine," Lady Minnaray said. "No need for such wide eyes."

"I'll be fine."

"I know you will."

Two of the other older sirens, Lady Minnaray's friends, gathered closer with reassuring words. "It's hard to believe it's already been three years since we chose you." "You and Dosia must be so excited!"

Every year, the village schools put on a weeklong festival where the children sang and displayed magic for the village elders. If the sirens and elders saw potential in any of the children, they would pull them aside for further testing, and a few fortunate girls were chosen to train as sirens. They were given a belt of enchanted gold, the links thin but impossibly strong and impervious to corrosion. For the next few years, the young sirens would learn to infuse the belt with magic, to tap into the magic when needed, and to enhance its powers as the years went by. By harnessing the magic outside themselves, their power grew. They learned the finer details of siren song, the power of their voices. And they would be warned, time and time again, of the danger of human men.

The trio of mermen singers finished, and Lady Minnaray moved toward center stage, gesturing for Esmerine to follow. The other older sirens took up the rear according to their rank. The audience was full of the faces of young sirens like Dosia, all smiling and welcoming. Esmerine clutched at her bead necklace, trying to stay calm.

"I present to you Esmerine Lorremen," Lady Minnaray said, her voice a song even when she spoke. "She has completed her training and is ready to take her place as a guardian of our waters."

An attendant brought out the ceremonial shell, as big as Esmerine's head, and opened it to reveal the golden belt Esmerine had spent so many hours filling with magic. Lady Minnaray lifted the belt by its clasps, and presented one end to Esmerine. For a moment, the belt was a chain between them.

Esmerine repeated her pledge after Lady Minnaray.

"I promise to serve as a daughter of the sea. For as long as I live, and it is within my power, I shall protect the sea and all its denizens from the human race, even if it means disregarding my own desires." Esmerine swallowed, remembering the day when the elder sirens explained how to wreck a fishing boat that took more than its share of fish and how to drown a human swiftly. She spoke the next words quickly; she wished to have them over with.

"The water is my mother, my father, my first love, and sworn duty. Should I have children, I will keep my belt safe for them, for the safety and strength of my people. With the donning of this belt, I give myself to the sea and its people forevermore."

How often had those words been spoken and then ignored? Esmerine wondered as she lifted her dark brown waist-length hair out of the way so Lady Minnaray could fasten the belt just below her navel.

"Now you are one of us," Lady Minnaray said.

"Well, you're a true siren now, Esmerine," her father said proudly. Her parents and Dosia were waiting for her when she left the center of the great room. The crowd was already beginning to disperse and resume conversations. "How does it feel?"

"Good." Esmerine didn't know what else she could say. Maybe it was impossible to achieve a great honor without feeling numb.

"Two sirens in the family," her mother said. "I would never have guessed it. Not a single siren in our entire family history, and now two! You girls are truly treasures." Not only did sirens bring prestige to a family, but even after death, a siren's belt was passed down through generations and could be used in times of need to work powerful healing spells or even defend the village. The status of Esmerine's family would be forever elevated from mere fishermen.

When Esmerine, Dosia, and their parents arrived home, Esmerine's youngest sister, Merramyn, was swimming to and fro adorning the cave walls with flower chains. Tormaline, usually the most serious of the sisters, was moving the magic lights to find the best position. Esmerine's mother swept in to interfere.

"Tormy, what are you doing? I said to put one in the middle of the room and—wait, where is the fourth?"

"*Mother*, we don't have a fourth." Tormy was thirteen, and lately she had taken to saying "Mother" in a particularly irritated way.

"We should have four. This one is ours, and I rented three."

"You rented two. You decided to save the rest of the money to buy sea bass, remember?"

Merramyn twirled through the water, draping the last flower chain around her shoulders. Dosia tried to take it from her. "Merry, don't be silly with that, you're going to damage it."

A flower broke free from the garland and swished around Merry's hair. She snatched it. "Dosia, look! Now you broke it! Mother, Dosia broke the flowers!"

As Esmerine swam out of the main room, she made a silent prayer to the sea gods that her family would make it through the evening without embarrassing her. Through the narrow door to the kitchen, her poor aunts were preparing food for a crowd with only one magic light to see by. The cave was old and had few windows, just small holes to keep water flowing in and big fish out. In wealthier homes, window nets kept out the fish *and* let in light.

Fragments of seaweed drifted through the water from the salad Aunt Celwyn was making, while Aunt Lia tucked bits of neatly sliced raw fish into empty seashells for presentation.

"Can I help?" Esmerine asked.

"Chase out this silly fish that keeps bothering me." Aunt Lia waved her hand as a slender fish darted past her face and into the shadowy corners. Just as Esmerine chased the fish out with the net, Dosia hooted a summons from the main room.

"The guests must be arriving," Aunt Celwyn said. "Go on and greet them! This is your day."

Esmerine raked her fingers through her hair, checking that her beads were still in place before she returned to the main room for hugs and congratulations. The guests arrived in a steady stream: her mother's friends, the fishermen who worked alongside her father, friends she and Dosia had made in school and in their neighborhood singing group.

She knew the routine from when Dosia had become a siren, and although she blushed and said humble things, she was secretly pleased to have a little piece of the attention Dosia had gotten for so long.

At dinner, her aunts brought the food around. Esmerine wished they had servants, particularly since her mother had invited Lalia Tembel and her family. Esmerine and Lalia had been casual friends for years now, but Esmerine had never forgotten how Lalia had teased her about playing on the islands and for her lack of bracelets when they were little. Lalia also used to tell Esmerine that if she spent too much time in human form she'd get stuck that way, and even when Esmerine had Dosia tell her off, Lalia had never apologized.

Still, her mother had not skimped on the food. They had the freshest fish, rare sea fruits sent from the Balla Sea, almonds and hazelnuts, enough olives that Esmerine had her fill for the first time in her life, and sea potatoes filled with minced shrimp.

They sang the Siren's Hymn in her honor, her mother's eyes growing red and wistful.

Come and hear the siren's call
Keep mankind in fearful thrall
As long as sirens guard the sea
All the waters shall be free!

Dosia, sitting beside Esmerine, squeezed her hand tight, and Esmerine knew she was thinking how wonderful it would be to be sirens together.

"Well, we ought to bring around the gifts, if anyone's going to sleep tonight!" her father finally said.

Esmerine received all the things she expected: necklaces of shell, a new brush and comb, the matched earrings and tail jewelry that had come into fashion lately—the last from the Tembels, of course, who wouldn't give anything less than fashionable even though Esmerine refused to pierce her tail fins and Lalia knew it. Her parents gave her the most beautiful bright-red headdress of beads to wear in her hair, much like the blue one Dosia had.

"I have a present for you too," Dosia said.

"Oh? But I didn't give you a present when you became a siren . . ."

"That's all right, because I'm older. And I have just the thing. Tormy and Merry helped me hide it."

Merry giggled and hurried to her sleep room with a flick of her tail that disrupted the table arrangements. Tormaline, who liked to think of herself as older than her years, folded her hands like she'd had nothing to do with any of it.

Merry came back holding a small figure in her arms, about one fin tall. Esmerine recognized it instantly.

It was a statue of a winged person, springing from a tiny pedestal into the sky, wings lifted. Dosia took it from Merry and tried to give it to Esmerine.

Esmerine didn't take it at first. She glanced, ever so quickly, at Lalia Tembel, whose brow had furrowed with amusement. Then her eyes moved to her mother.

"Dosia, what on earth is that?" her mother said. "Where did you get it?"

"It's a statue of a winged person," Dosia said matter-of-factly. "I found it in the scavenge yard."

"Esme, do you still like winged boys, then?" Lalia said.

"No," Esmerine said. "I never *liked* winged boys." Not that it was much better, liking what Alander had brought—books with worlds tucked between their pages, stories about animals that spoke and brave youngest princesses—always the youngest, Esmerine noticed, never somewhere in the middle.

"You were just jealous, Lalia," Dosia said. "Everyone wished they were friends with Alander back then."

"I certainly didn't wish to be friends with 'Alander,'" Lalia said. Her mother nodded as she spoke. "I'm glad we can trade with humans, but nevertheless, land people have a certain aroma, and crude manners to match."

"Alander smelled like books!" Esmerine said.

"Oh, *that's* appealing."

"I mean, *dry* books."

"Don't bother," Dosia whispered in Esmerine's ear.

"It is a very finely crafted statue," said one of her father's friends. "You could get a good price for that from the traders, all right."

Esmerine stuck the statue behind her with the other gifts, and only after everyone had gone did she finally take it to her sleep room and study it, half with her fingers, by the faint light of glow coral. The figure was unclothed, neither boy nor girl, and unlike Alander, it lacked personality. It was like those winged people she sometimes saw far in the distance, hovering on the wind, leathern wings stretched wide.

Dosia slunk into the room they shared, jabbing Esmerine's tail with her elbow in the dim light. Not only did the cave lack light, but it lacked space. At least they didn't have to share with Tormy and Merry as well.

"Now Lalia Tembel is going to think I have some sort of obsession with winged people," Esmerine said. The gift was a nice thought, but only Dosia had really understood her friendship with Alander, and Esmerine wished she had not made an example of it at the party.

"Who cares what she thinks?" Dosia said. "Anyway, it's a lovely piece."

That was true enough. The lines were smooth and graceful and realistically proportioned. It was the finest thing Esmerine had ever owned. "You really found it in the scavenge yard?"

"Well . . . not really. I found it in a garden."

"What garden?"

"Oh . . . outside of the village." Dosia was maddeningly vague.

"Were you with Jarra?"

Dosia laughed once, almost nervously. "No, no." She shifted close enough that bubbles tickled Esmerine's ear when she spoke. "Well, now that you're a siren too, I'll tell you, but you have to promise not to make a big fuss about it."

JACLYN DOLAMORE is also the author of *Between the Sea and Sky*. She spent her childhood reading as many books as she could lug home from the library and playing elaborate pretend games with her sister. She has a passion for history, thrift stores, vintage dresses, David Bowie, drawing, and organic food. She lives in Orlando, Florida, with her partner and three weird cats. She is currently working on *Magic Under Stone*, the sequel to *Magic Under Glass*.

www.jaclyndolamore.com

LOOKING FOR AN ESCAPE?

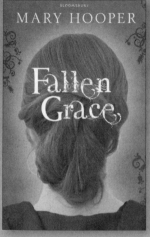
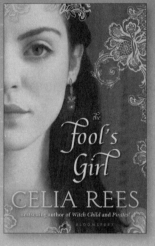
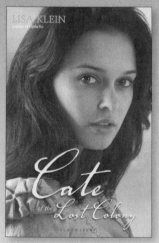
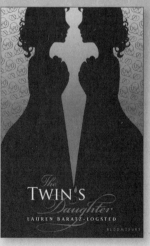

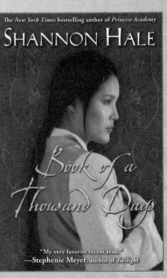